Other Bodies

Pro 31:89

Joel Ohman

whitefox Publishing Services

Printed by CreateSpace
First Printing, 2018

ISBN: 1981916849
ISBN 13: 978-1981916849

Cover Design by Ben S
Editing by Traci Finlay, TraciFinlay.com
& Jovana Shirley, UnforeseenEditing.com
Formatting by Jovana Shirley,
UnforeseenEditing.com

Because…
Because love lets live.
Because everybody matters.
Because we don't harm other bodies.
Because the body inside your body is not your body.
Because babies are babies whether they're inside or out.
Because babies are babies whether they're wanted or not…

Chapter One

Hot Sauce

Step forward, one foot at a time. Right and then left. Repeat.

Hattie felt a tiny tremor deep within, but—much like her judgment the night before—she quickly suppressed it.

She continued forward along the decrepit sidewalk, the dark-stained reds and browns of Philadelphia's classic row houses stretching along each side of her as far as she could see. Though one of the most famous landmarks in the entire country—the Liberty Bell—rested just blocks away, symbolizing freedom for all people, she had always thought it stood in sharp contrast with the overall disrepair down many of Philly's streets. More than just the Bell displayed visible cracks. Slender, spidery canyons yawned open along the long-neglected walkway before her; she stumbled sideways to maneuver around an especially large fissure. Why was it that she had known since a child how to avoid breaking her mother's back, but no one had ever bothered to explain to her how to avoid a broken heart?

She looked up, fighting the urge to close her eyes and sink to her knees, not caring who might be looking down from the lofty porches, silently inspecting her, judging her. And there were always people out on their porches. In many ways, this part of Philly was decades behind the rest of the country, but not all was bad; at least, around here, people knew each other. They didn't disappear into their garages, sliding in and out of their cars without ever knowing their neighbors' names.

Holding her neck stiff as a ramrod, eyes straight ahead, she continued forward. Part of her wished one of the chasms would just open up and swallow her whole. Where was a sinkhole when you actually needed one? She bit back an angry sneer. The sky looked like how she felt—mushrooming billows of dark clouds, the result of unknown pressures coming together in a turbulence of ominous, looming changes.

But that was nothing new. The sky that was, not her feelings; yesterday, she had dreams, a future, someone to love. Now—

A raven cawed, startling Hattie as it alighted onto a sagging telephone pole and then with an aggressive scream raced into the darkened skies.

Frozen mid-stride, Hattie sighed and took another trudging step forward.

Takers and profiteers had forever damaged their once-blue sky, and what remained was a dishwater-gray panorama of permanently cloudy atmosphere that seemed to stare sullenly back at whoever ventured a gaze heavenward. Not too different than what had been done to her, come to think of it, except it had to hurt worse because the taker who had hurt her had done so, claiming all the while it was an act of love.

But she knew differently now. It was easy to say you loved someone, but when you'd gotten all you wanted from them, would you stick around? If you just upped and left once you'd gotten your fill, then you were a taker, not a lover, full stop.

Her eyes looked skyward, but her thoughts were elsewhere. The thing was, she had thought he was the one. Wanted him to be the one. They had even planned for the future together. And, now, she saw his talk for what it really was. Just talk. Just a way for him to get what he wanted.

He had pressured her: *"Come on; give it to me. Why wait? What's the big deal?"* And the worst part: *"I want you so bad. I need you."*

But she had quickly discovered that giving in to his demands brought with it the knowledge that he didn't really want *her*, didn't really need *her*, but just her body. Once he had gotten what he wanted, the smug smile of satisfaction on his face had sent a horrifying flutter of fear tickling up her spine. The realization made her sick even now.

And the way he had just walked out after, discarding her like some used-up and worn-out commodity—that had hurt the most. She couldn't even take what little refuge there was in the lower impulse that he wanted her for her body anymore. It was as if her body was invisible to him now. Slowly, and then all at once, she had realized that the only body he was in love with was his own.

And yet the part she hated most: she still wanted him.

Tender hands caressing. Heartbeat pumping. Lips upon her neck, fingertips along her hip—the strength of the emotion threatened to pull her under, overwhelming her among its current. Images continued to flash across her mind like the flickering shades of a kaleidoscope, changing and distorting with the passage of time. But something real had passed between them; she had to believe that.

Her eyes hardened. Well, enough of that. The only person she could rely on was herself. She had forgotten that basic, essential truth—all for him—and look where that had gotten her. She wanted freedom, flexibility, the right to make her own way in the world, and she would. She didn't need him for that, never did.

Hearing voices ahead, she quickened her step and made sure to avert her eyes. This was not the part of town where strangers greeted each other with an easy smile and an exchange of pleasantries—especially if you were young and attractive. She fought back a bitter laugh; at least she didn't have any money to steal. She was broker than broke. But that would hopefully change after today. That was, if she could make it to her first day on the job without being late.

She cursed the moment of self-pitying indulgence that had caused her to miss her turn; she hated feeling like one of *those girls*—mopey, love-struck, and constantly rising and falling in an emotional roller coaster of feelings for this or that boy of the week. She wasn't like that, not at all. But then again, *he* wasn't supposed to be like those other boys either. Her face fell. Maybe she wasn't as different from them as she'd thought.

Amid an increasingly noisy chorus of chatter, a playful, musical voice called out above the din, "Hey, hey, hey, baby!"

Ducking her head, as if bracing against a stiff wind, she pretended not to hear and pressed forward, all thoughts and cares for her broken heart and her mother's back quickly discarded.

"Hey, come on now. Where you going in such a hurry?" The musical lilt took a dangerously abrupt dip, jarring like a clanging cymbal. "I know you hear me talking to you, so don't go ignoring me." He drew out the last words. "Look at me."

A shadow fell across her path, and she slowed to a stop, clutching her hands inside her jacket.

Slowly, she raised her head.

He was bigger than she was but not intimidatingly so. A jagged smile sliced across his face. "There, that's better." He paused a moment, his eyes sparkling as if sizing her up. "Not so bad, huh?"

She remained silent, keeping her face neutral and holding his gaze of smug superiority. With a start, she realized that, in sharp contrast to his burnt-mocha skin, his eyes were green. How annoying—this cocksure idiot was actually handsome. Wildly so. And, worse, he knew it.

He paused, an amused smile on his face, almost seeming to wait for her to realize this very fact about him and melt in the presence of his good looks. No doubt, he was accustomed to many women coming around to his assertive flirting for the same reason.

A spark of something untraceable flickered inside her, warmer than annoyance but hovering just under the temperature of rage. This wasn't her first rodeo with an unwelcome advance; she had learned early on you didn't tiptoe around horses you were trying to break; you acted quickly and aggressively to put them in their place.

Taking a step forward, she sneered. "What's *not so bad* would be you minding your own business." Taking another step, her hands still wrapped over her chest and inside her jacket, she spit out the words slowly and deliberately, "Now, get your sorry, worn-down pick-up lines back over on your porch where you belong, and get out of my way."

His eyes widened. She hated that, in that moment, she had to admit he really was uncommonly good-looking, and that made her feel even more annoyed.

"Well," he began slowly, the musical lilt back in his voice and the hint of a smile returning to his—full, gorgeous, perfect—lips, "maybe we got off to a bad start."

"Well, we're off to a great end." She moved uncomfortably close, pressuring him to step aside. "Nice *not* talking to you."

He laughed—a full, real laugh, deep from his belly, the laugh of the supremely self-assured, a man used to being in control of every situation, especially those involving women. Her hope that he would have bad teeth or some other hidden flaw turned out to be patently false when his perfectly even and perfectly white teeth gleamed like an ad for a toothpaste commercial.

He looked her in the eye, lips slightly parted. "I like a saucy woman." He raised an eyebrow appreciatively—no unibrow either, unfortunately. "And sauce you've got. In spades."

"Every man says that," she retorted. "Until they've got a little too much sauce on their hands, and all of a sudden, it becomes some kind of threat to their masculinity or something, and they can't handle it anymore."

His pupils widened, and he appeared speechless for a moment before that flat, shark-like grin returned. He spoke slowly, "It's not the sauce I ever have a problem with, believe me. It's just when the sauce starts to think it's the main dish that we have a problem."

Now, it was her turn to widen her eyes. She harrumphed; against her better judgment, she was talking to this conceited jerk. "And I suppose you think you're the main dish?"

He remained silent, his only movement a slight pursing of his lips.

She groaned. "Oh, please."

"Anyway, Hot Sauce, you still haven't explained why you're walking around in this part of town." His green eyes took on a predatory glint. "Especially alone. Saucy or not, pretty, young girls shouldn't be walking down this street all alone." He arched an eyebrow, eyes sparkling. "Especially with such a nice body."

Abruptly conscious of her own perfectly tanned skin and gleaming white teeth, Hattie frowned. She would not allow anyone to reduce her to just a body again. "Yeah, *my body*," she retorted, eyes flashing. "As in, *it belongs to me*, not some random creep ogling me on a street corner." Her mind returned to *him*—the other plunderer of her body and her heart—and her pulse quickened. "My body belongs to me, not to anyone else."

Lifting his palms high, he gave an amused grin, seeming to enjoy the interplay. "Easy now, Hot Sauce. I'm just saying." He tilted his head. "Baggage much? Is that why you're all alone out here?"

She suddenly realized just how close they were standing; she had moved close to try and brush by him, but he had remained in his place, looking down at her with that smirk that seemed permanently glued to his face. She swallowed, her throat instantly feeling dry, and she fought against the urge to lick her lips.

Taking a deep breath, she spoke with as confident of a voice as she could muster while trying to keep her heart from beating out of her chest, "I'm not alone. And I'll walk where I please, whenever I please, thank you very much."

He frowned. "Really, you're not alone?" As he swiveled his head, eyes roving around, the smirk returned. "I don't see any—"

Taking advantage of his momentary confusion, she forced her way past him, trying not to step on a crumbly piece of sidewalk. "Well, good talk. I've gotta go. Hope to *not* see you around." Even to her ears, it sounded a little harsh, but the curse of the very pretty girl was that you were hit on so often that it forced you to develop defensive forces and grow a hard-shelled exterior for repelling all the attacks. For a brief moment, she retreated; glancing over her shoulder, she blurted out, "You've got nice eyes though."

He stumbled back a step, appearing as equally caught off guard from her abrupt dismissal as her unexpected compliment. "Wait, where are you going? I don't even know your name—"

He grabbed her elbow, latching on with a grip more insistent than she liked.

A mistake.

Pivoting on her left foot, she withdrew her right hand from her jacket, and as delicately as a surgeon with a scalpel, she touched a small, blunt canister, no larger than a lipstick tube, against the side of his neck. He froze; she could feel his heart beating through the pulsing, ropy vein on his neck.

"I said I wasn't alone," she said softly. Again, this wasn't her first rodeo.

Slowly, he released his grip on her elbow.

For good measure, she pressed the canister roughly against his neck, depressing the skin enough to leave a mark, and then pushed away from him. "Don't ever grab me like that."

He frowned, looking genuinely confused. "I wasn't going—I mean, I didn't mean—"

She shook her head, walking quickly down the sidewalk as she slipped the little black canister back into the breast pocket of her jacket. Now, he knew; she was a child of the Philadelphia streets, just as he was.

"Don't care, and don't believe you."

"Ah, Hot Sauce, come on…" His voice was pleading, likely a novel tone for him. "I didn't mean anything by it; you didn't have to go all commando and whip out a prod." At this, his voice turned whiny, like a petulant child not getting his way. "And where'd you even get one of those things? I bet it's out of juice anyway."

"Wanna bet on it?" she hollered back.

Truth be told, the mini Taser might or might not have had any voltage left, but she could bluff with the best of them. A fault of hers that could, and often did, wind her up in trouble; she knew. Looking back, she could see him fingering the side of his neck and frowning, his full lips pouting. Squinting back over her shoulder, she could just make out a faint red mark on his neck.

"Nice hickey." The words tumbled out of her mouth without her thinking. Another fault of hers.

He looked up at her. "You-you gave me a hickey?"

His face was so quizzical that she couldn't help but grin.

"Something to remember me by!"

She turned away from him and jogged forward, bouncing lightly on the balls of her feet and weaving in and out of obstacles. Glancing back every so often, she could see the outline of his profile, still standing in the middle of the sidewalk and watching her fade into the distance.

She slowed her pace; she was almost to the street where she could cut over and get back on course, back into a safer part of town. Ever since the world had seemed to collapse in on itself, one had to be in a constant state of vigilance about which territory was currently safe and which might be gang-controlled, particularly here in Philadelphia.

She looked up at the always-bleak sky. Was it the environmental collapse that had triggered the governmental collapse or the governmental collapse that had triggered the environmental collapse? Either way, did it really matter? The long and short of it was that there were hungry, aggressive predators in the environment and in the government, and they were almost entirely focused on their own survival—to the exclusion of everyone else.

Now, they were here—in America still, technically, but as far as this being the *United* States, that was definitely a thing of the past.

Looking carefully left and then right before crossing the street—there weren't many cars driven by humans on the road anymore, but you certainly didn't want to find yourself in the path of an oncoming tank with its obstacle detection sensor turned off ... or worse, a fast-moving motorbike with its self-driving computer chip on the fritz ... or worse, piloted remotely by a band of teenage hackers looking for thrills—she hurried on ahead.

She thought back to the green-eyed stranger. In some ways, it was absurd—to go from thinking about *him*, the one from last night, to now this annoying—and annoyingly good-looking—stranger, all while so broke, she hardly knew where her next meal would come from. But she had come to realize that maybe this was just the human thing to do, part of what it meant to be human.

"Life hits us, and we just keep on going." Something her grandfather used to say. And *"life is still good, life itself is always good; we can always find something to be thankful for, no matter what unpleasant circumstance we find ourselves in."*

And she had added her own philosophical cap, more realistic than her grandfather's idealism: *You do what you have to do to survive.*

Stepping back onto the "safe" street, she breathed a sigh of relief.

Her grandfather had been a wise man; she realized this more now than when he was alive.

"Humans are survivors. We adapt, and we make the best of what we've been given. Life is a gift," and she would do her best not to squander it. Because today was a big day.

Her mind drifted back to last night, and she squeezed thoughts of *him* out of her mind; this was about her, about her future. She didn't need him. She finally had a job—no easy feat in this economy—and today was her first day.

Smoothing away nonexistent wrinkles, she brushed her hands across the front of her pants and took a deep breath. Here she was, the warehouse-like, nondescript building that lay virtually on the boundary line between the "good" and "bad" parts of town. She looked up at the small, innocuous-looking sign over the steel-fronted double doors: *Managed Motherhood.*

Closing her eyes and opening them quickly, she put on what she imagined was her best go-get-'em, capable, and disciplined nursing aide's smile and yanked the door open.

Chapter Two

Memories Never Play Fair

Hattie smiled hopefully across the desk. Even though they were both sitting, the other woman loomed over her. At first, Hattie had thought it was one of those executive power-play office layout strategies, where the chair behind the desk was placed significantly higher than any of the other seats in the room to give the illusion of power. But she now realized that Matilda, tasked with training her on her first day, was simply a large woman. A very large woman. Her throat suddenly dry, Hattie swallowed, watching Matilda's enormous, capable-looking hands trace information from Hattie's résumé as she mouthed the words aloud.

"Let's see, who did they send me this time? Hard worker. Dedicated. Disciplined. Of course, everyone says that." A snort that sounded suspiciously like a water buffalo escaped from her purple-tinged lips. "Now, what kind of relevant *experience* do we have here?" She was mumbling to herself and looking down at Hattie's résumé, clearly not expecting an answer. She grunted again and fell silent, scrutinizing the sheet of paper as if trying to unlock a secret code. Waggling her long-nailed, perfectly manicured fingers in the air, she abruptly began humming a cheerful little tune, almost as if Hattie were not even in the room, and then, with a frowning squint, she fell silent.

Hattie fought back the urge to fill the silence. Without warning, Matilda began to bob to her own internal rhythm once again. Eyes widening, she watched Matilda's head-bobs and shoulder-dips while trying to smother a laugh. Hands clasped on her lap and with straight-backed posture, she kept a tentative, neutral smile plastered on her face, masking the internal tumble of thoughts.

Did I misread the notice somehow? They said I'd already gotten the job, but what if it was all a big mistake?

She tried not to think of how little money was in her checking account. Her mind raced.

What if—

Matilda looked up, her face splitting into a wide, purple-lipped grin. "Okeydokey, I think I've seen all I need to see. I think you will make a great addition to our team here."

Hattie's eyes lit up and a tiny, hopeful smile stretched across her face, causing Matilda's eyes to sparkle in return.

"Don't worry; I just like to acquaint myself with all the new hires they send to us; we've gotten some real doozies over the years." She frowned. "And we hardly have any input in the decision anyway. I've only just seen your résumé right now." She added quickly, "But I really do think you'll do great; don't you worry about that. And you can relax now, my earnest, young job applicant. Sitting like that is making *my* back hurt."

At this, Hattie felt the blood rush to her face.

Paying no notice, Matilda spread her substantial arms wide, as if she were Moses parting the Red Sea. "You're one of us now. You're hired." Her voice was drawn out and soothing. "Relax."

A relieved laugh escaped from Hattie's lips, more high-pitched than usual. She forced herself to lean back in her chair, letting her hips slide forward. "Great, uh—thank you, I mean. I'm looking forward to it."

Matilda leaned back, now modeling full-on relaxation mode, the chair groaning under her enormous bulk. "So, we have a few minutes before the others get here, and then I can show you around our humble establishment. Why don't"—her broad, kind face, as quick as a blink, grew serious—"you tell me about taking care of your grandfather?"

Hattie started, caught off guard and fighting the urge to sit up straight again. "Oh, um, well—"

A big finger tapped the sheet of paper. "It's in your résumé. Caretaker for your elderly grandfather." She paused, eyeing Hattie carefully. "For five years. Concluding two years ago." She left the unasked question lingering in the air between them.

Hattie gulped, fighting back the swirl of memories. Stuffing them back into their neat little compartments—she was good at that—she focused on the task at hand: reply politely and respectfully, provide just enough information to not be off-putting, but keep things objective, unemotional, detached. As a teenager who had been living on her own the last two years, she knew the drill well.

"Well," she began, now sitting even more ramrod straight—she couldn't help it—"my grandfather passed away two years ago. And I was with him all the way to the end, to the very end." She looked at the space directly over Matilda's shoulder, her eyes growing glassy and distant. "I was all he had, and he became weak, very, very weak." Her eyes focused, and she met Matilda's sympathetic gaze. With a shrug, she spoke matter-of-factly, "So, I took care of him: bathed him, fed him. I did it all."

"I'm sorry."

Hattie cocked her head and paused. "I'm not. About taking care of him, that is. I'm sorry he died, of course, but he was old—eighty-three years old."

At this, Matilda's large, round eyes widened, and she nodded appreciatively. Even in the best of times, making it to that age was a feat. And this was most certainly not the best of times.

"It was time for him to go, and I'm glad that, those last few years, I could be there for him."

She paused, a long-dormant memory of her grandfather stacking cheese and crackers into a tower and then knocking it over with a cackle brought a clench to her stomach. She blinked her eyes rapidly, determined to take that memory out later and savor it, turning it over and over in her mind like a rare jewel.

It was funny how, sometimes, she could barely remember her grandfather's face; the first time this had happened, she had panicked, thinking herself a horrible person, maybe even possibly a psychopath. But, later on, she had come to realize it was just a natural part of absence, the way our minds worked. And, other times, she could dispassionately recall the events on the day of his death. But then, sometimes, a stray fragment of a memory, like the cheese tower, would come barreling out of nowhere and punch her in the gut so hard, she just wanted to cry out with the agony of it all. And then, quick as it had arrived, the feeling would be gone. Memories were like that: here and then gone, they'd sucker-punch you and never play fair.

Matilda looked up from politely scribbling what was probably nonsense on the paper in front of her— she was obviously giving Hattie a moment to get her thoughts together—and then smiled encouragingly at Hattie. "I understand," she said simply, her eyes endless glimmering pools that hinted at their own depths of sorrow.

"He was all I ever had, he practically raised me, and it was just nice," Hattie pursed her lips, fighting back another stray memory that certainly didn't belong in the here and now. "It was just really nice to be able to be all he had, to be there for him when he needed me." She lifted her chin. "I was glad to do it, to take care of him."

Matilda nodded, now speaking slowly, "I never really knew my parents either." Her voice was husky; she looked at Hattie, her eyes growing distant, as if seeing her but not really seeing her. "My grandparents raised me. They're gone now, but I would do anything…" Her voice faltered slightly before resuming its matter-of-fact tone. "I would have done anything for them."

Now, it was Hattie's turn to nod. An understanding passed between them—forgotten children left to find their own way through the tangled mess that was their feelings and their world, all in one. They sat in companionable silence for a few ticks of the clock.

"Well, it's about that time." Matilda placed both hands on her desk, lifted her eyebrows expectantly, and gave a smile so reassuring, it was practically maternal. "You ready to start your first day at Managed Motherhood?"

Hattie smiled in return, hopeful for the first time in longer than she could remember. "I'm ready."

"Let's go then!"

Following Matilda out the door, Hattie let her plasticky smile falter. At least she hadn't been asked how her grandfather died. She let out a slow, halting breath and repeated an internal mantra that, if she'd said it once over the last two years, she'd said it ten thousand times: *It's what he wanted, it's what he wanted, it's what he wanted.*

He had been really sick in the end; that much was true. But, as far as it being *his time to go*, well, it was more like the time of his own choosing. He had been in a lot of pain; otherwise she never would have considered it, of course.

But she had. And done more than considered it. Hattie had known that her grandfather wanted her to do it to ease his pain. That was the stock answer. But, deep down inside, in that little, itty-bitty secret place where no lies could penetrate, she knew the real reason. He'd wanted to do it for her. He hadn't liked being a burden to her; it had always been him taking care of her, not the other way around. She drew in a deep breath. But she had done what she had to do— nothing more, nothing less. It wasn't like she really had a choice. You just did what you had to do. End of story.

"Here we are—our first stop." Matilda glanced over her shoulder with a broad smile. "One of the most important places to remember—the break room."

Hattie ventured a laugh and gave a small wave at a young woman in scrubs disinterestedly tearing open an oatmeal packet in front of a grime-smeared microwave.

Matilda jutted her hip out, raising her voice to a level that made Hattie stop in her tracks. "Janet, let's get a move on, okay?" She twirled a long-nailed finger in a hurry-up motion. "You've been stretching your break out long enough."

Hattie looked wide-eyed at Janet, who nodded mutely, mumbling assent as she jammed the ripped oatmeal packet into a mug and placed it back into the cupboard before walking briskly by them, studiously ignoring Hattie's dumbstruck gaze.

As soon as the door closed, Matilda turned to Hattie, her face morphing into a bright smile. "Well, let's get going," she said cheerily, as if nothing out of the ordinary had happened.

Hattie nodded, swallowing the sudden lump in her throat. Apparently, Matilda had a mean streak. And, for some reason, she appeared to be on Matilda's good side, and she intended to keep it that way.

Chapter Three

The Button

"Will it hurt?"

"Oh, yes." His face turns somber. "Quite a lot, actually."

I swallow, fighting the urge to turn and run. "But it's worth it?"

He pauses, great golden eyes shining so brightly, I'm forced to squint. "It will help with the healing process," he says at last.

"But is it worth it?" I continue, pushing him for an answer I'm not sure he really has. "I just…" My voice trails off lamely. I'm delaying; even I know that.

He senses my apprehension, no doubt reading the worry lines I can already feel crinkling up my forehead, and his face softens into a slow, sad smile. "You want me to tell you it will all make sense in the end; I know." He meets my eyes. "You want to be reassured."

I nod. "Yes."

"But the choice has to be yours; you are free to choose, and when it's all said and done, only you will know." I can hardly hear the low rumble of his voice, so quiet, it's almost a purr. "You don't have to, you know. You can just stop right now."

"I know." But my mind is made up. I reach over and stretch the belt across my lap. "But I have to."

His voice grows more matter-of-fact. "I figured as much."

"Remember, you—" He chuckles. It turns into a deep-bellied laugh that sets his broad, expansive features aflame, his countenance seeming to refract all the glorious beauty and shimmering light from our surroundings. "Well, I guess you won't remember." He shakes his head. "You won't remember at all."

I smile. The joy of his companionship is something I wish I didn't have to leave behind, but his exuberance is contagious, and I can't help but catch some of his excitement. Not for the first time, I think maybe I'm more than a little crazy for wanting to leave this place.

He motions to my lap. "You don't really need to buckle the belt; it's more so just for looks."

"For reassurance?" I venture, a twinkle in my eye.

His eyes sparkle in return. "Sure."

"I'll take any reassurances I can get, false or otherwise," I respond, snapping the buckle into place with a definitive click.

He laughs again. "Okay." He takes a deep breath, the smile slowly fading from his features like the sun receding into the western landscape. "All you have to do is press the button then."

I close my eyes, holding them closed for a beat, and with a flutter of my fingers across the lapel of my shirt to smooth away nonexistent wrinkles, I slowly extend my fingertips toward the button.

It's red and dangerous-looking, a swollen knob protruding upward about the size of my fist. I pause, my fingers mere inches away, and incline my head in his direction. "Is this just for looks, too?"

Faint laughter burbles up from his chest. "Yes, but you do have to press it; it has to be your choice."

Nodding, I close my eyes again, and then I do what I've considered doing ever since I got here.

I press the button.

Chapter Four

Four Legs

The pounding grew louder, more insistent.

Hattie blinked, rotating to face Matilda, who just shrugged and frowned. "There they go again. I warned you it would happen eventually, didn't I?" Her wide, generous face seemed uncharacteristically annoyed. "Well, I guess a good first-day tour of the place should be realistic, huh? Give you a taste of the good and the bad of working here. They don't usually pick up steam until later in the day though, but I guess they've been starting earlier as of late."

Hattie nodded hesitantly and looked around. They were standing in the waiting room—a dingy, claustrophobic box with bad lighting that cast deep shadows along a mustard-yellow wall gouged with discolored spots and peeling plaster. A few well-worn magazines lay scattered along a disheartening end table—the most recent issue from so long ago, the date on the mailing label was worn and smudged. Still, she supposed that such timeless truths as "7 Ways to Look Flirty in Fall" and "How to Make His Jaw Drop: Seductive Secrets from the Stars" never grew old. Not a parenting or baby magazine in sight though, she noticed.

Hattie jumped as the pounding seemed to echo right outside the waiting room walls. She swallowed. "Are they ... close? Like, it sounds like they are right outside."

Matilda placed a hand on her substantial hips and wagged her head from side to side. "Oh, they're right outside—that's the truth—but they aren't going to be coming in here; you best believe that." Seeming to read the uncertainty on Hattie's face, her features softened. "They're just demonstrating; they aren't bad people." Her gaze darkened. "Not all of them." Her face brightened again. "And we have security." She glanced down at her wristwatch and frowned. "Well, usually. Charles is late. *Again.*" She snorted.

"Okay," Hattie said quietly. Looking from the sturdy-looking steel front door to the plated-glass receptionist area, complete with a protective retractable steel cover, she mentally pushed away the fact that even *not-bad people* sometimes did *very bad things*.

Following her gaze, Matilda spoke, "We do take precautions, of course. It really is rare that we have trouble from the Four-Leggers outside though. Usually, it's a woman with substance abuse problems or crazed family members with their own set of issues, usually psychiatric. Definitely the type of people we don't want getting any more children that they could just neglect—or worse, abuse. So, they are in the right place; this is right where we want them. We don't want to turn them away; we just need to keep them in check until we can help them. We put an end to any of that foolishness right quick though."

At this, the door jangled open, and a portly, good-natured black man toting a sack of fried cronuts flashed blindingly white teeth. "I come bearing gifts!"

Matilda sniffed, attempting to maintain a severe expression on her face, but gave up and broke into a smile that matched the man's exuberance. "Always the charmer, aren't you, Charles? Especially when you're late…"

He lifted the bag of pastries and winked roguishly. "And I always know the key to a good woman's heart, too." His eyes grew wide, feigning childlike innocence. "And who could fault a man who runs a few minutes late in order to bring sweets for his sweet?"

Matilda shook her head, reproving him with a playful swat of her large hand against his equally large shoulder. "Let's just see if you brought any of those chocolate-iced ones, and then maybe we can see about forgiving you."

With mock outrage, he jerked his head back. "Why, come on now, Tilly. *You know* that *I know* that those are your favorites, so"—he opened the bag with a flourish—"*all* I got was chocolate-glazed."

Matilda's face was practically glowing, and after Charles's theatrics, his considerable neck squished against his rent-a-cop security uniform, giving the appearance of a jolly, rotund caterpillar with rolls of chins that spilled over his collar.

Hattie giggled.

Turning toward the sound, his eyes lit up. "Why, who do we have here?" He nudged Matilda's elbow, already extended above the bag of treats. "Please forgive me. I was just so preoccupied with seeing my sweet Tilly here that I didn't even notice anyone else was in the room with us."

Jostling Charles with her hip, Matilda frowned coquettishly. "Oh, you stop it now, you hear?" She slowly licked frosting from a long purple nail in a way that said she very much didn't mean what she'd said.

Another tiny giggle escaped from Hattie's lips, causing Charles to break into an even wider grin. "Well, come on, Tilly, aren't you going to introduce us?"

Swallowing her bite, Matilda extended a hand. "Charles, meet Hattie. This is her first day, and she's getting a little tour around the place before we open up for business soon. She was just asking about the demonstrators outside, so we are glad you are here." She frowned playfully, pursing her lips and raising an eyebrow like a teacher chastising a naughty student. "Better late than never." She turned and smiled at Hattie. "And, Hattie, this is Charles, our security guard and resident ladies' man."

"*Ladies' man*!" Charles feigned outrage, clutching his chest as if shot. "You know I've only got eyes for you, Tilly." He lifted the bag of sweets suggestively.

Matilda rolled her eyes. "I'm fine, thank you very much, Charles. One is enough. They were delicious." As an afterthought and in a way that clearly spelled out the answer she was looking for, Matilda turned to Hattie, businesslike once again. "Hattie, would you like a cronut?"

"Oh, no. Thank you though." She smiled at Charles. "They look amazing though."

"Suit yourself." He jammed his hand into the bag, a look of glee on his face. "In that case, I will just—"

Matilda interrupted, her voice stern, "You will just head right back out the front door and make sure the walkway is kept clear for any early arrivals. That is what you were going to say, right?"

He looked up, hand frozen in the bag like a very large child caught with his hand in the cookie jar. Recovering quickly, he crinkled the top of the bag over and jammed it in one of his jacket pockets. "Of course, of course. Heading out right now." Wiping crumbs on his jacket, he glanced over his shoulder and shot a wink at Hattie. "Nice meeting you." He trundled back out the front door with a jangle, calling back, "Keep an eye on my Tilly. She's something special."

Matilda snorted, murmuring under her breath, "He's incorrigible." She looked at Hattie and shrugged. "Well, that's Charles."

Hattie smiled. "I like him."

Matilda turned from the door leading into the back and flashed a smile in return. "Me, too." She paused. "Well, any questions about up front here, in the lobby area? I know there's not much to see, and it's kind of run-down looking, but I'm sure you'll have lots of questions when we get back to the medical area."

Hattie paused, thinking. "Well, maybe one question." The pounding outside had died down slightly; no doubt Charles was working the crowd with his charisma as much as his bulk. "Well, never mind."

Matilda lifted her hand expansively. "No, please. Go ahead. Ask away."

"Okay." Hattie met Matilda's large brown eyes, seemingly a mile above her. "What did you mean by *Four-Leggers*? You called the protestors Four-Leggers and…" Her words poured out in a rush, and she started to feel the hot shame of asking a stupid question. "I just—never mind. It doesn't matter—"

"No, no, it does matter. It's a good question, and you need to know what you're getting into, working here." Matilda paused, her eyebrows knitting together. "The protestors outside are part of a wacko anti-choice group." She tilted her head, seeming to gather her thoughts. "I'm not sure what their real name is, but everyone around here calls them Four-Leggers, and they seem to like it, so even some of the media has started to use it." She looked at Hattie. "I'm surprised you haven't heard it before."

"I-I don't really watch much TV anymore," Hattie mumbled. She actually didn't have money for any of the newer devices, let alone a full-sized TV, but she didn't feel like mentioning that. "I don't really like to watch much." A lie. "I do like to read though." That part was true.

"Good for you." Matilda nodded approvingly. "Anyway, most of their signage says stuff like, *Not Four Legs* or *Two Bodies, Not Just One* or *The Body Inside Your Body Is Not Your Body.*" She motioned toward the front door. "If you listen closely, you can sometimes hear them chanting, 'Not four legs, not four legs,' over and over, so"—she shrugged—"we call them Four-Leggers."

"*Not Four Legs*?" Hattie asked, her brow wrinkling up. "But I don't get—"

Matilda nodded, understanding. "It's an old pro-life argument. Something like, every pregnancy involves two or more bodies: the woman's and the child's. Pregnant women don't grow two extra legs that belong to them, giving them four legs—hence, Four-Leggers. As in, 'Oh, really, you have four legs now? I don't think so.' " She looked at Hattie. "Those extra legs and arms and whatever, don't belong to the woman; they belong to the baby. It all started as a response to the old pro-choice slogan: *My Body, My Choice.* They counter that by saying, *The body inside your body is not your body.*"

Hattie blinked. "Oh, I see."

"It's a simplistic argument, of course." Matilda snorted, turning to the door at the back of the room. "I mean, we just talked about all those women hopped on drugs who come in here. What kind of life would any of those babies have, being born to a crackhead? What we do serves the woman and the baby. That's what those do-gooders outside don't seem to get." She shrugged her broad shoulders and held open the door for Hattie to follow. "It's a hard truth to hear, but sometimes, it's just better off for some babies to never be born." The lights flickered once, twice, and then fizzed back to full strength. Matilda looked up briefly and then motioned forward. "Especially in the world we live in."

"Okay," Hattie said, suddenly feeling small and very simple. The pounding outside began to increase in intensity again. "I'm coming. Right behind you."

Chapter Five

Congratulations

Working almost every day at MM gave Hattie a sense of purpose that was an inexpressible joy. She had thrown herself into the work, and though it was the usual monotony of a trainee, she found that she enjoyed the opportunity to lose herself in her work.

Now, weeks later, it was only when she stepped through the front door, the sturdy steel sealing shut with a whoosh of compressed air—the din around her suddenly twenty decibels quieter—that she realized she hadn't even been afraid to walk right through the middle of the protestors. In fact, she hardly even noticed them. Matilda had been right. Maybe after a long enough time, you could get used to anything; you could think anything was normal.

Hattie paused, looking up and nodding at the receptionist with a cheerful smile.

The receptionist, Sally-Anne, a greasy blonde with a gap-toothed smile, motioned for her to come closer. "Today's your big day, huh?" She placed her forearms on the counter, revealing matching sparrow tattoos on each arm. "You get to go back into the Medical Ring today, finally, right?"

Hattie shifted the weight of her overlarge backpack—she'd learned to pack a lunch and a book to read—sliding her arm out of the shoulder strap and walking closer. "That's right!" Her voice sounded weirdly perky, but she hoped she didn't sound nervous. "That's what Matilda told me yesterday, anyway."

Sally-Anne laughed. "Then, you can count on it. She practically runs this place; that's for sure."

"Yeah, I'm figuring that out."

Since meeting Matilda on her first day weeks ago, Hattie had come to realize that Matilda, while not a doctor, held most of the power in actually getting things done around the large clinic; the doctors were just the paid medical experts, sourced when a technological solution wasn't up to the task. It was a strange dynamic, not having real, human doctors around that often, and quite a departure from the stereotypical *arrogant and aloof doctors running the show* paradigm Hattie was used to from the laughably skewed medical knowledge gleaned from TV shows, but with all the recent technological advances, particularly in the OB/GYN field, it was the technicians operating the machines that seemed to hold most of the power. After weeks of seemingly non-medical related busywork training, today was finally the day when she could go beyond the foreboding metal doors and into the Medical Ring.

"She's great though," Hattie added hurriedly.

"Ha. Yeah, she is." Sally-Anne leaned back and lifted her chin toward the front door. "We know Charles certainly thinks so."

Hattie giggled and rolled her eyes. "I know, right?" She pointed to a box of pastries on the counter near Sally-Anne's elbow. "At least he's an equal opportunity charmer when it comes to the sweets."

"Mm-hmm, you know that's right." Sally-Anne made a shooing motion. "Now, get on in there. Don't wanna be late for your big day."

"Okay." Hattie smiled weakly, feeling a sudden spike of nerves dance like fireflies in her belly. "I'll talk to you later."

"Yep." Sally-Anne paused and then called out, "And, Hattie?"

Partway through the door, Hattie turned to see Sally-Anne's head already partially hidden behind the opened pastry box. Clearing her throat, Hattie lifted an eyebrow. "Yeah?"

Sally-Anne closed the lid, peeking over the box with a sheepish grin. "Um, I just wanted to say congratulations. Maybe you'll even be a nurse someday." She paused, brushing a strand of bleached-blonde hair behind a big-hoop-earringed ear. "That's what I'd like to do someday. Maybe both of us could be nurses together."

"Oh." Hattie felt tongue-tied for a moment before she managed to stutter, "Thank you. I really appreciate it." She adjusted the strap of her bag and then added, "And I don't know about the nurse thing, but I'd like that—working with you, that is."

Nodding, Sally-Anne sniffed and opened the pastry box again. Hattie took that as her cue to head through the door into the back.

Walking down the hallway, she pondered the clear hierarchy of medical versus non-medical, health staff versus support staff, and the different access levels for each within the clinic. While she was not a nurse, she was certified as an HHA, Home Health Aide, back from her time taking care of her grandfather. He had encouraged her to, "Make something good out of this for your future while you're here"—always thinking about others, even in the midst of suffering; that was her grandfather—so there was some overlap between what she had learned as an HHA and the skills needed as a part of the medical staff. Not to mention, being in Matilda's good graces went a long way to getting her access to the Medical Ring, an area that some support staff hadn't even been into, ever, some after years of working at the clinic.

Depositing her bag in the break room, she took a deep breath, smoothed the rumples from her scrubs, and headed out to find Matilda. Sally-Anne was right; today was a big day. If things went well, then congratulations were definitely in order because staff with Medical Ring clearance was eligible for a significant pay increase. Matilda had placed her large hand on Hattie's shoulder and informed her of this detail with a meaningful look. Hattie was a hard worker, she knew that, and the HHA certification was definitely helpful, but even she knew that she was light on any meaningful experience. She suspected that Matilda had sympathized with the story of her grandfather and was trying to take care of her in some way.

She paused in front of Matilda's office door, mid-knock. It did feel a little uncomfortable—the special treatment—but she certainly wasn't going to complain. For the first time in a long while, she wasn't flat-out broke. Still poor—that wasn't going to change anytime soon—but when that first paycheck had hit, she had danced a happy little jig in her small apartment. If she could just keep working, making a little money, maybe even saving some—doing all she could to keep busy and not think about *him* and what he had done to her weeks ago—then, well, she could finally see a way forward *without him*, and for once, the thought didn't make her heart catch in her throat.

She knocked on the Matilda's office door, quickly shutting down that line of thinking. The harder she worked, maybe the quicker her broken heart would heal. In some small but very certain way, she knew that she would eventually have to deal with what he had done to her that night. No, not like that; she had consented, wanted it even. But though she had consented to giving him her body, had she consented to giving him her heart if he was just going to leave with it and never return? She couldn't just suppress those feelings forever, but now was not the time. She had—

"Hey, there you are!"

Hattie turned around and saw Matilda walking down the hall toward her.

"All set for your big day?" Before Hattie could respond, Matilda, maybe noticing some apprehension on Hattie's part, spoke again, "And you're gonna do great; don't you worry about a thing. We're just going to do a little tour of the medical portion of the facility, check out some of the equipment, maybe introduce you around to some of the techs. We've got a pretty light schedule today, so really there's no rush, but maybe we'll even pop in on a procedure, too. You're gonna do great though—I just know it—so shake off those nerves, and let's get going!"

Hattie mustered a bright smile, trying not to feel overwhelmed. "Sounds great!"

Matilda paused, eyeing Hattie with big, sparkling eyes. "And congratulations! You might just be one of the youngest to gain Medical Ring clearance around here." She patted Hattie's shoulder, long, glittery nails sparkling in the fluorescent lights. "You just keep up the great work and keep learning, and you'll do just fine, honey."

"Thanks. I'll do my best."

"I know you will, honey. I know you will," Matilda answered, as if not really hearing her, and then abruptly turned to look over her shoulder. "Okay, off we go!" With a few businesslike strides away from her office, she whipped out a key card to swipe it into the Medical Ring, releasing the card to let the attached cord retract back to the clip on her waist with a *thwack*. She smiled back at Hattie. "Follow me!"

Hattie's eyes widened. The room they were in was cavernous—much bigger than she'd expected. Harsh fluorescent lighting buzzed over top of brushed and gleaming metal, the antiseptic cleanliness in sharp contrast to the general dinginess of the non-medical common areas to which Hattie was accustomed. Long rows of enormous machines were spaced throughout the room, housed in clusters with station numbers denoted above. Technicians and nurses moved with quiet efficiency, guiding patients from one station to the next with hushed murmurs, as if in reverence of the magnificent blinking machines that hulked over them.

Seeing the astonishment on her face, Matilda's smile grew wider. "Pretty impressive, huh?"

"It's … yeah, it's …" Hattie felt at a loss for words before suddenly blurting out, "It looks more like a server farm or maybe an automobile plant than a medical facility." Feeling foolish, Hattie lowered her voice. "I mean, it's just that, all the machinery—"

"No, you're exactly right." Matilda interrupted, seeming to enjoy the look of awe on Hattie's face. "And this is only our second-most impressive room," she said proudly before a shadow flitted across her face and made her smile falter.

Hattie frowned. "Oh, really? What do you mean—"

"Oh, nothing," Matilda spoke quicker. "Nothing at all. I'm getting ahead of myself. I was just bragging about our facility a little." She paused, circumspectly eyeing her reflection in the gleaming brushed aluminum of an expensive-looking machine almost her height. Picking at the corner of her lip with her pinkie fingernail, she turned back to Hattie and spoke calmly, her eyes level, "Just saying, you should see where the fetuses go after they leave this room, but enough about that already. I talk too much."

"You mean, that—" Hattie turned her gaze to Matilda, who was now toying with her hair and looking away from her, seeming to inspect the floor. Was Matilda hiding something? "The fetuses are taken from this room to—"

Matilda lifted a hand, her face showing a spasm of annoyance. "We'll get to the womb room later on, but just wait until you see what we have in *this* room."

Hattie's stomach flip-flopped. Matilda was a nice lady, but in that moment, seeing the change morph across her face, she had to remind herself that she was first and foremost her boss, not her friend. Intuitively, she knew Matilda, underneath the fun-loving exterior, was not someone to be trifled with. But what was the womb room? And why did she seem so secretive about where the fetuses were taken?

Before she could continue that train of thought, Matilda waggled a perfectly plucked eyebrow. "And"—she lifted a long nail—"we even have robots!" At this, her voice hushed, as if the robots were listening, which, Hattie thought, maybe they were, given how far voice recognition had come over the years. A vague sense of unease settled in. Matilda nodded to Station 8 in the left corner of the room. "Just watch. We'll wait here for a moment, so we don't interrupt their routine." She glanced down at her wristwatch. "Just give it a moment. It should be any second now…"

Despite her edginess, Hattie felt a growing excitement. What exactly was she going to see? She had watched enough sci-fi movies to have a wide visual vocabulary of what might appear. With the amount of sophisticated technology in this room alone, anything from a cyborg with a humanoid appearance to a miniature droid seemed within the realm of possibility.

"And here we go." Matilda pointed. "There it is!"

Reflexively, Hattie giggled. It was quite large, a cylindrical canister that slowly rolled and rotated in a precise sequence of choreographed starts, stops, and turns. Looking closer, Hattie could see that the top had a clear, bubble-like helmet, almost like a space suit, from which patients could look out. Seeing lifelike eyes looking out made Hattie fight the urge to jump before she realized that they didn't just *look* lifelike; they were, in fact, lifelike eyes because they belonged to the person inside the bot. The eyes passed right over her though, giving the impression that Hattie could see in but the patient couldn't see out. She frowned. It was still unnerving.

Matilda laughed, enjoying the look on Hattie's face. "Kind of gives you the creeps at first, huh? Seeing those eyes looking out…" She placed a hand on Hattie's shoulder. "Don't stare now though.

That's a real person in there, a patient, and unless they have their player on, then they can see you, too."

"Oh, right, okay." Hattie pulled her eyes away. "Their player?"

"Each of the T-E-Ds—Transport and Examination Devices, we call them TEDs—are equipped with full panorama, 360-degree 4-D viewers. It's all built right into the bubble helmet glass, so most of our patients are watching an interactive movie or just trying to relax with an immersive beach environment or some other soothing experience that we have cued up."

Hattie blinked, looking closer. "Wow. So, they are essentially Segways with an enclosed exterior shell."

"That's it! That's exactly right. What a perfect explanation!" Matilda clapped her hands together in delight. "But that's just the Transport part—still, pretty cool. And you might have even seen these types of interactive gaming rigs out in the consumer market before—"

At this, Hattie nodded. She had heard of them. Not that she had ever set eyes on one. They were wildly expensive. And not without risks, if she remembered correctly. They were so immersive and realistic that, sometimes, people would forget to come back to reality until they were an emaciated, former shell of themselves. One guy in Japan had even withered away to nothing and died.

"But the Examination part, that's where it gets exciting." Matilda's eyes were shining, the sign of a true tech lover, which, despite her appearances, Hattie thought probably had to be the case if you were to advance in this type of cutting-edge clinic. "What we've done is essentially take one of those high-tech gaming rigs and then outfitted them with all the latest and newest in body-scanning technology."

"So, they don't even realize they are being scanned…" Hattie wondered out loud. A far cry from the old TSA airport body scan days.

"That's right!" Matilda spoke hurriedly. "They have to give their consent ahead of time, so they know they are going to be scanned at some point, of course."

Hattie turned back to the TED with new eyes. It might not look like much, but there was a lot going on under the hood. "Right, of course," she spoke softly. "But they don't even have to panic during the scan or become uncomfortable."

Hattie knew that these immersive gaming rigs could mimic virtually any body sensation: relaxing at a beach, climbing a mountain, even exercising at the gym. Unfortunately, when they'd first hit the market, they had been in the news primarily for the body sensations of the more carnal and salacious variety. Hattie blushed. It was certainly a testament to their power though.

"It's genius," she said softly, still looking at the innocuous machine busy about its predetermined route. It was amazing, truly. They had single-handedly eliminated one of the biggest fears people had when visiting a medical facility. No wonder abortions—and profits—had been climbing so rapidly at Managed Motherhood in all the latest news cycles and, in turn, stirring up more of the old-school protestors and demonstrators like the Four-Leggers.

"It really is." Matilda nodded in agreement. "But here we are. At least there still needs to be *some* human workers around." She laughed, running a long nail along a stray strand of hair. "And here we thought that the robots would come and take all our jobs. Well, thankfully, that didn't happen." She laughed again at the irony. "They just took *most* of them."

Holding her hand up, motioning for Hattie to stay put, Matilda looked at her watch for a moment and then looked up with a smile. "Okay, we're all set. Let's head on over to Station 8." She nodded to the TED now sliding with a click into the dock at Station 8, its human inhabitant now ushered into another TED by two soft-spoken aides, nestled against another suite of big, expensive-looking machinery, and then said, "We try and adhere to a pretty strict schedule around here, so one of the most important things to learn is that we, the humans, should respect the preprogrammed schedules of our robotic coworkers. We all work together here, and each one of us, robot-kind or humankind, deserves to be treated with respect."

Hattie spoke softly, her voice tiny in the large space, "Oh, I see."

Walking briskly to Station 8, Hattie close behind, Matilda gently patted the smooth fiberglass shell of another TED docked at Station 5. "It's never an issue of danger. All of our TEDs have very sophisticated sensors, so you don't ever have to worry about one running you over or anything. But, after the Artificial Intelligence Personhood Act, and then the Artificial Intelligence Discrimination in Employment Act a few years later, we have to take appropriate steps to treat our robotic colleagues with respect, and a big part of that is just not getting in their way." Turning so fast, her sneakers squeaked on the floor, Matilda stood directly in front of Hattie.

Hattie slid to a halt, backtracking a step to keep from ramming into Matilda. Still, Matilda pressed closer, cutting her off. Feeling her heart rate spike, she looked uncertainly up at Matilda, still standing motionless and expressionless in her scrubs, her wide hips blocking Hattie's way.

With a quick smile, Matilda took a step back. "Sorry, I know that was uncomfortable, but I do that demonstration for everyone's first time into the Medical Ring." She lifted an eyebrow, her eyes dancing. "Not really fun, huh? Having someone all up in your personal space, keeping you from doing what you need to do."

"No," Hattie admitted, her beating heart returning to a normal tempo.

"Well, it's easy for us to think about the TEDs and other moving machines around here as *just* machines, but if we are constantly getting in their way and ignoring the important jobs that they have to do—well, you wouldn't like it if one of your colleagues constantly did that to you, would you?"

Hattie looked closer at Matilda, waiting for her to burst into a smile with the punch line, but no. She was serious. "I guess I never really thought of it like that."

Hattie looked at the TED docked in Station 8 as they resumed walking forward. It made a strange kind of sense. More and more jobs were being destroyed by automation than ever before; there was hardly any job around that a machine couldn't do better, so there was certainly economic justification for treating them with respect. And, if there was one thing about the way the world worked that Hattie had figured out, it was this: where there was an economic or financial incentive for something to happen, it would inexorably happen, without fail.

"Well"—Matilda wiped a speck of dust off the TED so gently, it was almost a caress—"here we are. Station 8." She waggled her eyebrows. "The fun part of the tour."

For some reason, this made Hattie's heart beat even faster than before. "Okay, um, great."

"Just you wait, just you wait. This is the best part," Matilda murmured as she tapped commands into her phone that she had withdrawn from her scrubs. With a soft whoosh of hydraulics, the TED withdrew from the dock, and the front part of its exterior retracted to reveal an interior lined with what looked like deflated balloons. "And here we are! So, beach or mountains? I'll warn you though; they've added an adventure pack add-on to the mountain option. You're actually hang-gliding through the Rockies for part of it, a great way to spike your heart rate for some of our tests though."

Matilda's eyes were bright, and despite the trepidation Hattie felt, she got the sense that Matilda would love to hop in there in her place if she could.

Seeing the look on Hattie's face, she quickly added, "All perfectly safe though, honest."

"Um, I'll try the mountains," Hattie said shyly. "I've always wanted to hang glide."

"Excellent. I knew there was something I liked about you!" Matilda tapped a few more commands in her phone, her lips pursed in concentration. "Okay, all set!" She motioned to the TED. "So, if you will just step right inside. I know there will be a lot of extra room for a pretty little thing like you, but"—she rotated her substantial hips from side to side in a quick merengue step—"these TEDs are one-size-fits-all, so … it will be roomy at first, but as soon as the shell retracts, all those cushiony-like things will begin to inflate. You might feel a little claustrophobic at first, but just try to relax. The feeling passes really quickly once they make contact with your skin. And then I will already have your mountain hang-gliding experience keyed up, so from there on out, just enjoy your trip!"

"Okay." Hattie licked her lips and stepped forward. Reaching with a tentative hand, Hattie touched the smooth fiberglass shell of the TED gently, cautiously. She had been in some tight places before—hidden in some tight places before—and never felt claustrophobic, so of that, she wasn't worried. But she had never been mountain climbing, let alone hang-gliding before—she'd never even been outside of Philadelphia!—so she had no idea how her stomach would react. Gulping, she got the sudden picture of her losing her breakfast in the small, enclosed space and ruining all the expensive equipment.

Seeming to read her mind, Matilda urged her forward with a gentle touch of her lacquered nails. "It will be okay, honey. Honest. These are the latest generation models. It was only in the very first couple generations that there were ever any issues with vertigo, motion sickness. Now, that's practically unheard of. You'll love it."

"Don't I need to sign a release or anything?" As soon as she asked the question, she regretted it for the stalling tactic it most obviously was.

"You already did." A knowing smile split Matilda's face. "Didn't you read your welcome packet?"

Hattie grinned sheepishly. "Oh, okay." She tucked a stray strand of hair behind her ear and stepped forward. "Well, here goes." Stepping into the TED felt very much like stepping into an upright spacesuit. Looking out and down at Matilda, now positioned up higher and taller than she was, she gave a tiny thumbs-up.

"Okeydokey, have fun!" Matilda's excitement was palpable. She tapped on her screen and then looked up, eyes bright.

The exterior slowly wrapped around Hattie, sealing her into a cocoon. A cocoon that felt as if it was slowly compressing inward. Her heart fluttered with alarm.

"Do not be alarmed," a soothing female voice intoned over the internal speakers.

Ah, TED is a woman.

For some reason, Hattie found this funny, and the initial stress of the moment caused her to giggle. And then, just as quickly as it'd started, the feeling of compression was gone, and she felt herself suddenly lifted into the air, the bracing bite of crisp mountain air whipping against her face. She closed her eyes and could swear that her hair was streaming out behind her, although on some level, she knew her hair lay closely against her head, sweaty and stuck between the compressed sensor cushions.

She opened her eyes, and the view took her breath away. She darted and dipped among the clouds, already airborne over snowcapped mountain peaks, sometimes dropping so low that she had to fight back a tremor. They surely wouldn't program a mountain crash, would they? She hated to think what would happen if the software glitched. She wondered what would happen if she did crash; her body might be safe against the cushions, but it was so real, maybe her mind would crash. Warm sunshine caressed her face, and she turned upward, basking in the rays. She felt like a hawk, an eagle, soaring free and unhindered among the clouds and the mountains. She had always loved the city, loved Philadelphia, even with all its danger and problems—it was simply all she had ever known—but now ... now she knew why people would flee to the wilderness, a return to nature, and a refuge from all that had gone wrong in the cities.

At first, tentatively and then with more confidence, she extended her arms wide, feeling secure in the harness of the glider. She screamed with exhilaration. Was this real? Was she screaming in the TED, and Matilda could hear her, or was it just in the simulation? It wasn't like she could really move her arms out wide like that in the TED, or could she?

At one point an actual bald eagle screeched a challenge, drifting along beside her on a wind current, giving her a fierce side eye before swooping away. She took a sharp intake of air, not realizing she had been holding her breath, and began to suspect that the crisp, mountain air—yes, she was certain now; it had to be—had an actual smell to it. She could even *feel* the temperature dipping as she skimmed closer to the glistening mountaintops, the sunrays from above warming her back while the soft, downy snow beneath her churned up in a crystallized flurry that chapped her cheeks. Somehow, all of her senses were being activated. She knew that one's sense of smell played a crucial role in the sense of taste, and she suddenly remembered hearing about a company that claimed to be able to deliver "VR food" and now could totally understand why.

Eventually, she gave up on questioning the process and just embraced the seeming reality of the virtual reality. This wasn't virtual reality; this was, for all intents and purposes, *reality*.

And then it was over.

She fought the urge to scream out, *No!*

But, instead, she just calmly waited for the exterior to slide open, the little balloon-like cushions slowly deflating to give her space. She would never look at drab, grimy Philadelphia the same way again.

Stepping out, a buoyant expression her face, she turned to face Matilda, still standing in the same spot. Had it really only been minutes?

Matilda looked up from her phone, a flustered look on her face. "I-I'm so sorry. On your welcome packet, all your paperwork, I never should have let you go in there without knowing what you were signing. Oh, I'm so sorry. I didn't know." She was babbling now, very out of character, and even glancing around somewhat wildly as if she might be in trouble.

"Didn't know what?" Hattie asked slowly, feeling a chill settle in her bones.

"Oh, I'm sorry. Now, I'm making it even worse, aren't I?" Matilda tapped her phone, slipped it into her scrubs, and then walked forward, placing an arm around Hattie's shoulders.

Hattie pulled back, frowning. "Making what worse?" she asked. "Just tell me."

"Oh my. This is the worse training session ever. Exactly what *not* to do." Matilda smoothed down the front of her turquoise scrub pants. "Okay, you need to know that in the welcome packet documents you signed, you consented to a *full* and *comprehensive* TED experience and evaluation."

"Okay…" The frown lines on Hattie's forehead deepened. "But what does that—"

"And part of that *full* and *comprehensive* evaluation is a pregnancy scan, much earlier detection than what you can buy in a store and much more reliable, too."

A funny little twinge deep down inside made Hattie feel even colder, the feeling spreading like ice water through her veins. Now, she really couldn't help but think about *him*, about what *he had done to her heart* on that night almost three weeks ago, but *his* face was all she could see. She looked up at Matilda, unseeing and unbelieving.

"I'm sorry, honey. I'm so sorry." She met Hattie's eye. "It shouldn't be this way; I know."

Suddenly, the contrast between the clean mountain air in the simulation, the landscape bright, full of sunshine and possibilities, and the dingy and dangerous, crime-ridden streets of Philadelphia hit Hattie like a punch in the gut. She stiffened her spine. "I need to hear you say it."

Matilda swallowed, her eyes depthless pools of sadness and joy all in one. "You can do this though. Maybe it's a blessing in disguise—"

"Please," Hattie interrupted, feeling her knees go weak. "Just say it."

"Congratulations," Matilda said, accepting Hattie's small body as she crumpled against her. Stroking her hair, she whispered softly, "You're pregnant."

Chapter Six

No-Brainer

The knock startled Hattie awake. Blinking her eyes rapidly, she bolted upright in bed. Light streamed in through the window over her bed. *Did I sleep in and miss work?* For a moment, that was her biggest problem, and then her face fell as she remembered. Why she was home, in bed, at ten on a Tuesday morning. After Matilda's revelation yesterday— Hattie's hand drifted unconsciously to rest on her midsection—Matilda had hastily, guiltily told Hattie to take a day off. Never mind that she had needed the money; she had been too stunned to respond.

The knocking sounded again on her front door, escalating to full-on pounding. Rotating her feet over the side of the bed, she groaned. The only person who police-knocked on her door like that was her landlord, Big Sean.

As if intruding in on her thoughts, his gravelly voice barked out, authoritative yet bored-sounding at the same, "Hattie, I know you're in there. Come on out." A pause and then another shout, "I talked to Maya. She said you haven't left for work yet."

Gritting her teeth to keep from yelling out her opinion of the nosy old crone she had for a neighbor, she half-jumped, half-fell out of bed. Standing up crookedly on one foot, she tugged on some pants from a tangled heap on the floor and shuffled toward the front door, calling out, "I'm coming."

Smoothing an errant flop of hair across her forehead and grimacing at what her bedhead must look like, she opened the door, plastering a smile on her face she didn't feel. She forced a bright note of cheeriness into her croaky morning voice, pretending she was a morning person and had been up and productive for many hours. "Hi, Big Sean."

"You're late," he said, his round face impassive. "I need my money." As usual, getting right down to business. He stood in her doorframe, an enormous hulking mountain of a man, baggy clothes hardly disguising his great bulk, though she knew him well enough to not feel intimidated physically. He didn't talk much, but he was generally honest—as far as inner city slumlords went, that was. Maybe owing to the way he had gotten his start. It was common knowledge that he'd started out as rent collector for the previous landlord and then had worked out some kind of deal to take over some of the depressed properties the previous landlord no longer wanted. He slouched to one side, as disinterested in her as a bear in a mouse.

She attempted a flutter of her eyelashes but found them annoyingly stuck together because they were so sleep-encrusted.

He frowned. "You got something wrong with your eyes?"

She ignored him and doubled down with a white lie. "Good to see you."

He remained immobile, his only movement a slight tipping of his chin as if to say, *And? You know I'll wait here all day if I need to.*

And he probably would, she thought. She swallowed uneasily. Feeling flustered at his dead-eyed nonresponse, she finally sighed. "I'll have rent to you by this afternoon," she mumbled, knowing that to pay him today meant no money left for groceries for at least the next three days until her MM paycheck hit.

He nodded. Turning away, he stopped and looked back, another frown creasing his face. "Why aren't you at work? Thought you got a job."

"I—" Hattie faltered. A sharp bite of panic took her breath away at the memory of yesterday's revelation, but she quickly tamped down the feeling and forced another smile. "I do, I do. Today's just my day off." *Oh, by the way, I found out I was pregnant yesterday. Isn't that great?* Another sliver of panic trilled up her spine. How could she possibly take care of a baby right now? It wasn't like she could just skip on paying for diapers and baby formula and child care and the million other little expenses she was probably forgetting. But if she skipped out on paying rent …

She swallowed, meeting Big Sean's intent stare with a hesitant smile.

"Okay," he said slowly, brows knit together in suspicion. He shrugged. "This afternoon," he said with finality, turning again to leave.

"Right. I will." Hattie said, leaning against the doorframe for support. "Thanks, Big Sean." Her voice was tiny. "Bye."

He turned his broad back to her and lumbered away, ignoring her and heading to other more important matters.

She stepped back and slowly shut the door.

She looked around her apartment, her mind racing. In reality, even if she went without a much-needed stop at the corner store, she was still a little short on rent. Last month's rent. She swallowed, forcing herself to think. She would figure something out; she always did. Breaking down or crying wouldn't change a thing.

Her eyes rested on an end table, the only nonessential piece of furniture she owned, standing on flimsy, crooked legs and abutting the tattered old sofa. She had long-since pawned the TV and all other frivolities to avert similar crises in previous months.

How much could she get for the end table?

Not much. Not enough.

She tread heavily back to the bedroom. Almost before the conscious thought reached her, she found herself slowly emptying clothes from each dresser drawer. Well, at least she wouldn't have any reason not to just throw her clothes on the floor. She looked at a pile of crumpled shirts already in the corner with a wry grin; not all that much would change. A bitter laugh burbled up before she choked back a tiny cry.

She could remember a time when she had been shocked to find out that a neighbor down the street had nothing but a dresser drawer for their newborn baby to sleep in.

Baby cribs are for rich folk, was the answer she got in response to her young, wide-eyed stare.

Her face fell. Now, she couldn't even afford a dresser drawer for her baby to sleep in at night. What kind of mother would that make her?

Sinking to her knees, she began withdrawing clothes from the bottom drawers. For a moment yesterday—one daring, hopeful moment—she had decided to keep the baby. Chubby, glowing cheeks. The first coo of *Mama*. Snuggles at night. Someone to hold and to love. Someone to talk with and share secrets with as they grew older. Someone to live for. Someone to remind her of her grandfather.

She set an old, faded pair of pants gently on the floor and stared, unseeing, at the holes and rips. She squeezed the fabric in a balled-up fist and then released her grip with a tiny cry. In some small way, it was like she was being offered everything that had been missing the last few years.

A family.

Someone who would need her.

And someone she would need, too.

But the momentary illusion passed. She looked down at the empty dresser drawer. It would be ridiculous for her to have a baby right now.

She got to her feet, relishing the need to focus on the upcoming business transaction; at least this was a problem she knew how to solve. She eyed the now-empty dresser.

Didn't take long to empty out when you didn't have much to put in it, she thought wryly.

Well, she'd likely get enough to make rent this afternoon, plus some left over for groceries. It would be easy enough to turn into cash; she knew a guy. Melo, right down the street. He paid people upfront and would even haul it away for her. She knew that, obviously, he'd be selling it for more than he paid her for it, but he was usually fair enough; he had known her grandfather. And, when you needed the money now, what choice did you have? Funny how all the rich-people advice went out the window in a crisis situation. What they never seemed to realize was that, when you had nothing, everything was a crisis. But the important part: she'd be good for one more month.

Taking a deep breath, she walked out her front door, her feet pointing toward Melo's as if by their own accord. But her mind wasn't on furniture. Everything came back to the baby. It always did. She took another step forward, a long sigh escaping her lips. It was an easy decision. A no-brainer, as her grandfather would have said. Of course she couldn't keep the baby.

Or could she?

Hattie walked forward uncertainly, the usual spring in her step resigned and plodding and, for once, not even bothering to avoid stepping on the cracks. She sometimes walked the neighborhood when she needed space to think, and she found her mind returning to its usual routine.

A saying her grandfather often said: *"Hard doesn't mean impossible."*

She shook her head slowly, fighting back tears at the image of her grandfather's intent gaze, as clear as day, trying to teach her dismissive, young self a life lesson. He had repeated his instructions to her early and often, taking his role as her parent and caretaker seriously, probably thinking all his wisdom was going in one ear and out the other.

But she *had* listened.

And, even now, she could hear his voice in her head—calm, patient, but imploring.

"Hattie, listen. This is important."

Oh, how she wished she could go back in time, listen to him. Truly listen. Let him know how much she needed him. Still needed him.

"Hard things are hard, Hattie. I'm not denying it. But, listen, this is important. Hard doesn't mean bad. Good things are hard, Hattie. Some of the best things in life are hard."

Suddenly, she saw his comments in a new light. It couldn't have been easy, taking care of your tiny granddaughter, especially as a frail old man, but he had never shirked that responsibility. Had loved it even. She never once heard him complain, never once heard him talk down about her parents.

Tears welled in her eyes, and she continued walking forward, her vision blurring. It was hard, sure, but they had had a good life together.

"It's all about choices, Hattie."

"Hard choices, easy life. Easy choices, hard life."

"Remember that, Hattie."

"Remember that."

Oh, how she missed him. He would have known what to do.

The chatter of young children brought her dilemma into clearer focus. The high-pitched wail of a child's voice drove a stake of doubt into her heart, but then, as a group of grimy, frantic little boys, no older than seven, careened around the corner of a house, their gleeful shouts interspersed with the sibilant sounds of mimicked machine gun chatter. She looked closer at the shirtless boys' protruding ribs, their grease-streaked, ill-fitting clothes—one boy was wearing just one shoe, and it looked to be a good three sizes too big—she forced herself to make the responsible decision.

The world was hard, even for those with resources. And she had nothing. Sure, she finally had a job, but how long would that last once she had to take time off for the baby and then child care? They might not fire her outright, but she knew how these things worked.

We've had to do some reorganizing. It's not about you, or the baby, of course. We're just heading in a new direction.

And, even if she could stay on, by some miracle, who would watch her baby? How would she even pay for food? Government assistance only went so far, ever since the budget cuts, and she had heard enough stories from friends that the women's shelters and church food pantries were only a short-term solution. Besides, she could barely afford to feed herself, let alone another human being entirely dependent on her. And then there was medical care, clothes …

The sense of panic was wild and frantic, yet still she walked forward, tamping it down. She shook her head slowly, her gaze bent downward as she continued on, the shrieks and chatter of the playing children receding behind her like the fading wisp of an alternate history, a dream of a better future.

The thing that bothered her most though, the thought that made her breath catch in her throat, was, she kept picturing her grandfather's face. He might say it was a no-brainer, all right—he loved to use that phrase, his face wild-eyed and incredulous—but he would demand that her only option was to keep the baby, she knew that much. And it wasn't just conjecture; in a moment of infrequent transparency, she had come right out and asked him what he would do if she were to get pregnant. He had paused, a look of shock on his face, as if seeing her as a woman for the very first time, trying to fit the idea of his beloved angel of a granddaughter as a pregnant teenager into his mind and not succeeding.

But then a big smile had creased his worn features, and his beard had waggled with glee as he said, *"Why, I'd be a great-grandfather! And a sexy one, too! What we'd do, of course, is celebrate!"*

Tears welled in her eyes, and she quickened her pace. Well, there was no celebrating now. Her grandfather was gone and, along with him, what fragile support system she used to have. Now, it was just her.

And, if she had realized anything, it was this: not only was it just her, but it was also *all up to her*. She was all she had. And when it was just you—when your back was up against the wall and the ever-present suffocating anxiety of not knowing where your next rent payment was going to come from was bearing down on you like an anvil on your chest each night as you slept—well, you just simply did what you had to do, and there was no apologizing for that. She refused to feel badly about that. She was a survivor, always had been.

"Watch it!" she yelled, kicking a stray soccer ball that another pack of wildly hooting young boys had errantly tumbled across her path from across the road. "Stay away from the street!" she snapped, looking past the little snot-nosed jaywalker who picked up the soccer ball with grimy fingers and furrowed his brows in Hattie's direction before darting back to his friends.

Head high, she marched forward without a backward glance.

If she wanted to take charge of her own life, be a responsible and productive member of society, then she certainly couldn't do that by falling into the stereotype of the inner-city teenage mother. She wanted to make her own way in the world, not stay at home collecting food stamps and scrounging for baby formula.

She didn't *want* to have an abortion; she just *couldn't* have a baby right now. There was a difference, right?

Sure, people talked a lot about choice, but what if, sometimes, you just didn't really have a choice? Her doubt about being a good mother, her broken heart about the baby's father—all of that was purely an exercise in theory. In the real world, you just did what you had to do to survive.

She pushed thoughts of her grandfather and hard choices out of her mind and turned the corner, lifting a hand as Melo popped up off his front porch step in recognition, an enormous gold-toothed smile plastered on his face. He seemed to have that uncanny ability of all smooth-talking wheeler-dealers to sniff out a good deal from a mile away.

Her gaze hardened, and she forced her chin up. Taking a deep breath, she willed a smile to appear on her face and found that, somehow, it had. Laughing so as not to cry, she accepted his eager bear hug, biting back a sharp inhalation of Old Spice as her face pressed into his neck. She would do what she had to do. Her grandfather would have understood.

Chapter Seven

Special Treatment

Hattie collapsed into the break room chair, the chance to finally stop standing on her aching feet making the cold metal feel like a recliner. She stared, unblinking, at the sad little granola bar on the table in front of her. It had been a harder adjustment than she'd thought, spending all day on her feet and without much more than cronuts and granola bars to subsist on. She enjoyed the work, but she was so busy, she hardly had time to think, let alone stop for a proper lunch break. Really, it was a blessing, in some ways, since she couldn't afford a proper lunch anyway.

Sally-Anne poked her head in the door, scanned the room with a roguish look, and flashed Hattie a mega-watt grin. "Come on, Hattie. Let's go!" She stepped in the door, jewelry jangling, and made a hurried motion. "Follow me. Got something I want to show you."

Hattie groaned. "I'm on break."

Sally-Anne's face brightened. "Exactly. That's why I came to get you now. Me, too!" She drumrolled on the door excitedly, waggling her hips to the beat. "Let's go, let's go, let's go! Come on, trust me."

She hopped up, jamming the granola bar in her pocket. "Okay, okay, okay." She allowed Sally-Anne a weak smile, which only served to encourage Sally-Anne into doing a fancy two-step and twirl, features aflame with enthusiasm.

"After you." Sally-Anne made an exaggerated bow and opened the door for Hattie with a flourish. "Just wait. You'll be glad; just trust me."

Hattie shook her head, fighting back a smile. She was incorrigible, but she certainly made a long workday more exciting. "How do you always have so much energy?"

Grasping Hattie's shoulder, Sally-Anne grew serious. She took a deep breath, looking up and down the hallway as if on the lookout for eavesdroppers. She met Hattie's eye. "Cronuts," she said, her face deadpan before she snorted, dissolving into a fit of laughter.

"You're ridiculous." Hattie giggled, succumbing to Sally-Anne's silly mood. "Well, I haven't exactly been skipping out." She patted her stomach and had a sudden flash of *what else* was still inside her, and then her hand slowly dropped. "I guess I'm not doing it right," she finished weakly after noticing Sally-Anne's knitted eyebrows.

"Guess not," Sally-Anne said at last, her hand dropping from Hattie's shoulder. Her lips twitched. "You'll learn though. The key is to ingest a cronut at least once every hour. That's the secret."

"Ah, okay." Hattie nodded, walking beside her down the hallway and grateful to not have to meet her eye. "Makes sense. I'll have to increase my dosage."

"You'll learn; you'll learn." Sally-Anne stopped and turned to Hattie, eyes wide. "Speaking of increasing dosages, did you see Matilda flip out on Annette? That was some serious level-ten-thousand beast mode. I thought she was going to fire her on the spot."

Hattie swallowed, remembering the scene yesterday. Annette—another new hire, a quiet, mousy-haired brunette who had such an unfortunately masculine nose that some of the others had taken to calling her Man-nette—had made a mistake, disregarding the printed instructions Matilda had provided for an IV, and attempted to administer the dosages by memory. When Matilda had found out, she had gone ballistic, railing on poor Annette until there were tears in her eyes.

"Hattie?" Sally-Anne prodded. "You saw that, right? With Annette?"

"Yeah," Hattie replied, fighting the urge to look over her shoulder for Matilda. It was testament to just how severe the browbeating Matilda had handed out that Sally-Anne felt sorry enough to call Annette by her real name. Hattie nodded. "I saw."

Sally-Anne blew out a long exhale, nodding her head slowly. "That was rough, even by Matilda standards."

Guiltily, Hattie murmured something unintelligible. She had, thankfully, never personally encountered Matilda's legendary nasty streak, and she had the sneaking suspicion it was because of their shared sense of bonding during her first interview and Matilda's guilt about what had happened in the Medical Ring. Hattie's hand slowly drifted to her stomach before she realized what was happening and made an effort to walk naturally, hands swaying by her sides. She wondered if anyone else had noticed the special treatment.

"Not that you'd know." Sally-Anne snorted. "She *loves* you."

"Well, um …" Hattie stammered. So it was obvious. "I don't know. I've never had a problem with her."

Sally-Anne rolled her eyes. "Whatever, Hattie." Her eyes brightened, and she came to a stop, gesturing to the door ahead. "Here we are."

Hattie swallowed, fighting a sudden twist of her stomach as she realized where they were. "The Medical Ring," she said slowly.

"Yep!" Sally-Anne exclaimed. "Now that Matilda's given you access and shown you around, it's time for the *real* tour."

"Oh, I don't—" Hattie bit back her reply, blinking her eyes rapidly. "I mean, I'm not sure Matilda would want—"

"Oh, please, Hattie." Waving a hand flippantly in the air, Sally-Anne bumped the access card on her hip against the sensor and then pushed the door open all in one fluid movement. "Don't be such a worry wart."

Hattie stepped across the threshold, the gleaming immensity of the room bringing back a swirl of memories that made her heart beat wildly in her chest. Absurdly, she wondered if the baby could feel her spike in heart rate, and she quickly pushed the thought out of her mind. Hearing only the quiet thrum of machinery and seeing no human movement in the entire cavernous space, she frowned, coming to a standstill behind Sally-Anne's scampering form.

"But where is everyone? It's the middle of the day. I don't understand—"

"Come on, Hattie. I told you to trust me." She looked back over her shoulder, flinging a greasy flop of bangs with a head bob and a wink. "Everyone's in training, Matilda included, for at least the next hour. We're cool, really."

"But what if someone comes back—"

"Hattie," Sally-Anne interrupted, turning to face her, hand on her hip. "Seriously? Since when did you turn into such a killjoy? I should have just asked Mannette already, sheesh."

"No, it's just—" Hattie mumbled, her eyes coming to rest on Station 8, the unit where she had soared across mountain vistas only to discover—

shaking her head, she forced a grin at Sally-Anne's impetuous figure. "Nothing. Sorry. Just tired, you know. One of those days."

In a flash, Sally-Anne's face bloomed back into an enormous smile. "Oh, believe me, I understand. Don't worry about it at all." She clucked sympathetically. "But come on. This is going to cheer you up." She inclined her head, thankfully away from Station 8 and over to Station 12. "Over here, I want to show you something."

Hattie followed wordlessly, doing all she could just to keep her breathing slow and steady. Station 12 looked identical to Station 8.

"So, beach or mountains?" Sally-Anne asked. "With Matilda, which one did you choose?"

"I—"

"Wait," Sally-Anne interrupted with an uplifted hand. "Let me guess." She crooked her head, staring at Hattie intently. "Beach. Definitely beach."

Hattie grinned. "Nope."

"Wow, really?"

"Yep." Hattie smiled at the memory. The hang gliding really was amazing. "I've always wanted to hang glide."

"Okay, now, we're talking! That eagle—crazy, right?" Sally-Anne gave an approving nod, a smile playing across her features. "I knew there was a reason I invited you instead of Man-nette."

Hattie rolled her eyes. "Whatever."

"But"—Sally-Anne lifted a finger and an eyebrow, excitement lifting from her features like hot steam off summer pavement—"have you ever raced in the Indy 500?"

Hattie pursed her lips, lowering her chin. "Every week," she said, deadpan.

"Well then, great!" Sally-Anne gave a saucy flip of her hair. "Maybe you'll be able to keep up with me then." With a few expert taps of her nail against the touch screen, she gestured inside. "Here, you take Station 12. I'll go hop in Station 11 and sync us up."

Hattie stared into the cushion-filled interior, her mind picturing Matilda's stricken face the last time she had been here in the Medical Ring and suddenly realized her palms were sweaty.

Congratulations.

You're pregnant.

Her heart beat faster and faster, a runaway locomotive threatening to veer off the tracks at any moment.

Sally-Anne cocked her head, a quizzical expression on her face. "Getting some pre-race nerves? You won't get any motion sickness or anything; don't worry. It'll be just like the other day with Matilda." She grinned. "Just *better*, of course. No health scans, no *treat the machines as people* lectures." Seeing Hattie look up in surprise, Sally-Anne laughed. "Oh, yeah, you think you're the only one to hear that? Matilda likes to give that lecture to everyone, stand all up close and in their business to prove her point. But, anyway, none of that boring stuff. *This* will be *fun*, Hattie; trust me."

Hattie closed her eyes and took a deep breath, opening her eyes with a smile that was not a reflection of her roiling stomach. "Okay, let's do this. What do I do?"

Sally-Anne clapped her hands together. "That's what I'm talking about! Just hop in and get ready to drive. Simple." She lifted a haughty eyebrow. "Simple to drive anyway, not to beat me; that's impossible. I'm the red car. Just look for the one way out in front of you."

Hattie shook her head, glad that Sally-Anne's incessant chatter gave her overworked mind something else to focus on beside the *extra* passenger she would be taking into the VR race car with her. Settling back against the already inflating cushions, Hattie called out, "I hear a lot of talking, but I don't hear your engines revving yet."

Sally-Anne laughed with delight, and as the panel closed around her, Hattie could see Sally-Anne hurriedly scurrying over to her own TED unit at Station 11.

Closing her eyes, Hattie took in a deep breath of air and then slowly exhaled. With a jolt, she began to rock side to side, the insistent whining of high-octane engines all around her like lathered thoroughbreds straining against the reins.

Her eyes popped open.

She sat low to the ground, snugly harnessed into some kind of super-performance race car that yowled like a caged animal wanting freedom.

Oh. She looked down and hastily removed her foot from the pedal she had been mashing. The ferocious scream immediately changed to a throaty, menacing growl. Okay, she must be in neutral, just waiting for the race to begin. She looked up and a tiny blinking indicator arrow on the steering wheel gave her shifting instructions, the only clue that this reality was virtual.

Just as she was marveling at the tang of gasoline in the air, the pitch of the crowd around the track began to rise, thrumming with excitement almost as loud as the crescendoing engines, she heard TED—once again, a woman's voice—speak in her ear, "Depress clutch. Depress clutch."

Looking down, she quickly pushed the leftmost pedal.

"Depress gas."

Without waiting, Hattie jammed her foot against the gas pedal, simultaneously flicking the paddle shifters on the underside of her steering wheel.

Sally-Anne was going down.

In what seemed like mere seconds, the two pace laps were over, and Hattie found herself screaming out along with the crowd as she rocketed forward, weaving in and out of the other vehicles as if they were standing still.

All of them, that was, except for a pesky red car that hung next to her as if glued to her side. She chanced a quick glance over and found herself looking at Sally-Anne's windblown face, cheeks rosy with excitement. Startled, she took her foot off the pedal for a moment. Could Sally-Anne see her right now, too?

Taking advantage of her surprise, Sally-Anne darted ahead, now firmly in the lead and putting some distance between her and Hattie. Eyes narrowing, Hattie grasped the wheel and hammered the gas pedal again. With an answering roar of her engine, she closed in on her, drafting behind Sally-Anne's red vehicle as they swooped around each curve.

For a brief moment, she was jolted out of the virtual reality as she felt a car physically ram into her from behind, causing a brief flash of panic that she would spin out of control and slam into the wall. Her eyes widened, seemingly frozen in time as her car skittered sideways, tires biting into the track with a squealing sound as they struggled to gain purchase. She felt g-forces tug her back against her seat, the breath catching in her throat. Even though this was so-called virtual reality, the effect on her body was no less real, wasn't it? Should she even be doing this simulation while pregnant? She had a sudden, desperate need to curl her arms around her stomach and protect—her features fell; what was she thinking? She had already decided to abort; why did she even care now?

And yet she did.

She shook her head, using all her willpower to focus on the race. Her tires hugged the track at last, course-correcting just in time to veer back down a sloped curve and stick her directly behind Sally-Anne. The movement, the motion, the jolting and swerving—this couldn't just be in her mind, could it? If she concentrated hard enough, she thought she could faintly make out the sensation of the TED unit whirring and screeching in "real life" along the Medical Ring floor. Of course—she nodded, understanding, even as she raced along the track to the roar of the crowd—it wasn't 4-D just as a marketing gimmick; she felt as if she was moving because *she actually was moving*. She thought back to her Segway comment to Matilda, and the realization made her smile.

All of a sudden, just as they were nearing the home stretch and Hattie was gearing up to make her move on Sally-Anne, everything went dark, and she drew to a stop, motionless but sweaty-necked and breathing hard.

The panel slowly opened, revealing the harsh fluorescent lights of the Medical Ring.

And Matilda's frowning face.

"Sally-Anne!" Matilda's voice rang out, echoing through the cavernous space and causing Hattie to shrink back. "Come out here right now."

Sally-Anne's voice was small and so uncertain, Hattie almost didn't recognize it. "Yes, ma'am. Coming."

Matilda sighed, turning back to Hattie. "You, too, Hattie. Come on out here."

"Okay," Hattie said, quietly ducking her head as she exited the TED unit. "Sorry," she mumbled, feeling foolish, like she was the teacher's pet caught playing hooky or vandalizing the school or doing some other juvenile act.

"Oh, I'm sure you were just following Sally-Anne's lead here." She extended a long nail at Sally-Anne. "And she knows better."

Hattie interrupted. "No, it's my—"

Matilda lifted a palm. "Now, now, I'm sure you're wanting to be a great friend to Sally-Anne and claim it was all your idea, blah, blah, but I know better." She smiled archly. "Might I suggest instead that you consider whom you befriend a little better next time?"

Hattie gulped, unsure of how to respond.

Matilda blew air through her lips in exasperation. "Hattie, you're free to go." She paused, a tiny smile playing across her features. "Just"—she put her hand on a jutting hip—"next time you girls decide to race in the Indy 500, invite me, okay?" Seeming to delight in the twin looks of shock on their faces, Matilda shook her head. "At least that will give me an excuse to get out of all these meetings. That is, if you two aren't scared to face off against Purple 58 and be left in my dust."

Sally-Anne's jaw dropped. "Wait, that's *you* in the simulation? I thought I was playing against the computer all those times; you are *fast*!"

"Of course I am," Matilda responded haughtily. "That's my all-time high score you're racing against. Who do you think helps test out every new software pack we get in here?"

Hattie found herself smiling, easily recognizing once again Matilda's love for new technology.

"Wow." Sally-Anne nodded her head appreciatively. "I never would have thought that—"

"But that does *not* give you the right to just barge in to the Medical Ring anytime you want for entertainment purposes," Matilda interrupted, her lips pursing. "We try to keep things fun around here, and I look the other way when the lab techs organize some fun events with the TEDs. They are amazing machines—I get that—and we've even found some bugs in the new simulations that way, so it is worthwhile, but we are here to *work*, Sally-Anne; do you understand what I'm saying?"

Nodding furiously, Sally-Anne's hair bobbed along with her jangling hoop earrings.

"Okay, you two can leave."

Quickly, Sally-Anne grasped Hattie's elbow, and they hustled toward the door, their sneakers squeaking on the floor. "Told you you're her favorite," Sally-Anne whispered. "If you weren't here, I would have been blasted worse than Man-nette."

For the first time, Hattie realized why Sally-Anne might have been so insistent on her coming, too.

Matilda's strong voice called out. "And, Sally-Anne?"

Turning in unison, Sally-Anne still grasping Hattie's arm, Sally-Anne called out, "Yes?"

"Swing by my office on the way to reception. I've set out some extra filing for you."

Sally-Anne stammered, "Oh, okay. Should Hattie help with—"

"Just you will be fine."

"Oh, okay. I'll get right—"

"Thank you. Move along now." Matilda turned away from them. "That will be all."

As they walked down the hallway, hurriedly putting some distance between them and Matilda, the Medical Ring, and any other assignments she might decide to levy on them, Hattie tuned out Sally-Anne's mumbled complaints. She knew now, for certain, that she was receiving special treatment from Matilda, but what she also knew was that it wasn't just because she was her *favorite*.

It was because she was *pregnant*.

That look in her eye, the imperceptible softening of pity, the darting glance to Hattie's midsection and back up to her eyes, so rapidly that Hattie had to ask herself if she had really seen it. But she wasn't just imagining things. She knew that now.

If she had the baby, was that what she had to look forward to for the rest of her life? She was someone to be pitied, someone to be looked down on, a pariah—a poor, single mom in a difficult situation. Could it get any more cliché?

All the innocuous utterances: *I don't know how you do it, all by yourself. You're so young.*

Translation: *You can't do it. You're too young.*

She nodded a silent good-bye to Sally-Anne as they parted ways at Matilda's office door.

"Don't mind me doing all this extra work while you go back to your break." Sally-Anne rolled her eyes but then flashed a quick, conspiratorial grin. "We'll finish our race next week; don't worry. If you can hang with me, that is."

Hattie snorted, shaking her head at Sally-Anne's irrepressible gumption, and made a shooing motion as she walked away with a smile. At least Sally-Anne wasn't about to give her any special treatment.

Chapter Eight

No Other Choice

Taking a deep breath, Hattie knocked again, this time like she meant it.

The sound of shuffling came from inside, and the curtains parted just a sliver to reveal an eye intently watching her. Hattie waved timidly, lifting her hand quickly and placing it by her side, feeling foolish and wondering why she had decided to pay a visit to Mrs. Tonnetti after all these years.

As the chain lock jangled on the other side and the bolts retreated with a *thunk*, the door swung slowly open. Hattie resisted the urge to sway, like a child uncertainly leaning from one foot to the other, though she felt once again like a ten-year-old girl coming to beg for some pizzelles—the best cookies in all of Philadelphia.

Mrs. T, as all the neighborhood kids used to call her, lifted the top knob of her cane a few inches into the air in greeting. "Haven't seen you in a while. Haven't been making cookies in a long time, you know." She never was one to beat around the bush. She leaned against the doorway, still in her nightgown, opened and closed a wrinkled, age-spotted hand, and winced. "Arthritis."

"I know; I'm sorry." Hattie felt a wave of guilt wash over her.

Ever since her grandfather had—was gone, it had just been too difficult to stay in contact with even some of her closest neighbors, those people who had known her grandfather for decades.

Seeing them was like seeing little parts of her grandfather—the way he would talk about cars with Mr. Polonowski out in front of his faded red row house. She always got a butterscotch candy from him, and even though she used to hate them, now, they were one of her favorites. And the way her grandfather would snatch a still-cooling cookie from Mrs. T's counter, evading her playful swats with his usual flirtatious banter, making her eyes light up and look a remarkably twenty years younger. And it was just too hard for Hattie, so she had withdrawn, hardly ever going outside. They had all come by, of course, to show their respects, comfort her, offer to help any way they could, but eventually, their visits had slowed and then stopped entirely. That was just the way it was.

But, now, here she was. Older, alone, and pregnant on Mrs. T's doorstep. She looked into Mrs.

T's deep brown eyes, still bright and sharp despite her frail and hunched exterior, and burst into tears.

Eyes softening, Mrs. T extended a skeletal hand and grasped the crook of Hattie's elbow. "There, there. Come on inside. I've got some pizzelles from Sarcone's in the cupboard still—not as good as mine, but edible." She shut the door and then led Hattie over to a plastic-wrapped sofa. "Sit. I'll be right back."

Hattie collapsed, sinking into the soft cushions, the stickiness of the plastic seeming to suction her rear like a Venus flytrap and absorb her slowly into its pillowy bowels. Thankfully, her feet finally reached the ground—one welcome change from the many times she had entered this room as a child. She was older, a *grown-up* now, and yet she still couldn't resist the swirl of memories walking into this room had dredged up.

She looked at the walls, crowded with memories and knickknacks. And that was what all those tchotchkes really were—memories. Ever since childhood, she had marveled at why anyone would choose to keep so many random objects around their living space—a wooden alligator from a trip to Florida (Mrs. T had hated it, claiming she couldn't return from the humidity fast enough, something that seemed strange to Hattie since all Mrs. T did was complain about Philadelphia's weather), a tiny flag of Italy (standard for many homes in this neighborhood), and even a small clay snowman, dry and brittle with age that Hattie herself had given Mrs. T as a little girl. But, now, Hattie understood. After her grandfather had left, she had clung to every reminder of him she could. It wasn't the same; she knew it wouldn't bring him back, but when someone you loved left, you took what you could get. Hattie wiped away tears as she smiled.

Mrs. T set a small china plate of cookies on her lap. "You remember that snowman, huh? You gave that to me, you know, as just a little girl."

Hattie blinked away tears, chomping into one of the crunchy, almond-sweet, waffle-like Italian cookies and found herself transported ten years back in time. "I-I just can't believe you still kept it. After all these years."

Mrs. T eased herself into her recliner, plastic crinkling as the chair accepted her small frame. "I wouldn't dream of getting rid of it. You gave that snowman to me on a day when I really needed cheering up." She looked at Hattie steadily, leaving unspoken the fact that she was now doing the same for Hattie. "You were a precious little girl." She gave a little snort. "Mischievous but precious. I …" Her eyes grew weary and she looked at the wall as if deciding whether to speak before finally turning back to Hattie. "I miss your grandfather a great deal, too. He was a good man."

"I know," Hattie said quietly, looking down at her cookies. "Me, too."

"So, what brings you to my doorstep, Hattie? I know it's not to reminisce with an old lady like me."

Hattie felt a pang of guilt. She wasn't the only one hurting after her grandfather died. Why hadn't she realized that there were others feeling the same way right around her and that maybe they needed her and she, them? She took another quick bite, giving herself time to think. *But that's what grief does; it blinds us to the pain of others and turns us in on ourselves, depriving us of the very antidote our aching hearts need.* She knew that now. *Hurt concealed festers while hurt revealed heals.*

"I, well—" Hattie tried to swallow, the cookie seeming to turn to chalk in her throat. "The thing is that—" Finally, she swallowed, clearing her throat. "I'm pregnant," she said. *Mrs. T is a straight shooter, so why beat around the bush?* She held Mrs. T's sharp-eyed gaze. "I'm pregnant," she repeated quietly, as if convincing herself, too.

Nodding, Mrs. T sank back into her chair. "I see." She pursed her lips and gave another tiny nod. "So, you're not dying of the cancer or anything; that's good." She allowed herself a small nibble of her cookie, licking her lips like a fastidious mouse cleaning its whiskers. "You had me worried for a moment there, showing up on my doorstep and all worked up."

Hattie blinked rapidly. "Well, yes, but—"

"And the father?"

"Not in the picture," Hattie said quickly, adjusting to Mrs. T's no-nonsense, direct approach and finding that it was a welcome relief from everyone at the clinic who tiptoed around the subject, as if Hattie couldn't be trusted to have a pragmatic conversation. "He's not around anymore. He's just— well, he's just gone. And he's not coming back." Hattie's lips felt dry—and not from the cookies.

Mrs. T frowned. "I take it he was the one who always used to come around? With the big, shiny smile and—"

"Yes," Hattie quickly interrupted, feeling her face bloom with color. It wasn't as if anyone else had been over; she wasn't some kind of floozy with men in and out of her house. And, apparently, Mrs. T saw more out of her curtains than Hattie had thought. "It was just him."

"Hmm, I see." Her old, weathered face grew thoughtful, and then she abruptly met Hattie's eye. "And what did he say when you told him?"

"Told him?"

Mrs. T lifted an eyebrow. "That you're pregnant with his child."

"Well, I didn't exactly tell—" Hattie felt her pulse begin to race. "I mean, he left, so why should I, you know? It's not like he deserves to know. He left."

Mrs. T shrugged in that way of the elderly not understanding the youth. "He left, but it's still his child as much as yours."

"He's gone." Hattie bit into another pizzelle, the cookie crunching with a satisfying finality.

Mrs. T held her gaze for a moment and then nodded. "And the baby? I suppose you're not going to keep it."

"No, well, yes, I mean—I mean, yes, I'm not going to keep it." Hattie felt the blood pounding in her head. "I mean, I just—it's not like I—"

"You have no other choice," Mrs. T said matter-of-factly. "Smart girl."

"I guess, yeah. I can't really take care of it all by myself and so ..."

"Very sensible." Mrs. T took a sip of her tea, and they continued on to talk about their neighborhood, Hattie's new job.

"Guess you won't have any trouble taking care of your little situation then," Mrs. T said, as if discussing car repair.

Mrs. T's common-sense approach, had, in turn, shocked and then reassured Hattie. Inexplicably, her mind drifted back to a story her grandfather had told her once about his mother, Hattie's great-grandmother.

Her grandfather hadn't grown up in Philly—at least, not his entire life; he had been raised out in "good Amish country," alternately known as the "Pennsylvania boonies," somewhere near the endless farmers markets and rolling fields of Lancaster, Pennsylvania, where it was more common to see a steel-wheeled tractor than a stop light, and you were more likely to hear the clip-clop of a horse pulling a buggy down the road than to hear the honking of an automobile horn.

He'd told the story once, of being a young farm boy watching his mother calmly gathering a litter of newly-born kittens, cinching them up in a burlap sack and drowning them in the river before resuming her substantial workload of morning chores. There were too many mouths to feed on their little farm already, and so the baby kittens had to go; it was as simple as that.

Hattie had cried herself to sleep for a week after hearing that story. She knew her grandfather had instantly regretted telling her upon seeing the look on her horrified face, as if he had revealed to his beloved granddaughter that his mother had been some kind of psychopath who hurt young animals for fun instead of a hard-working, sensible farm woman who did what was necessary. But, eventually, Hattie had come around to realize that, even though horrible things happened, there was a vastly more horrifying truth about the world she was growing up in: sometimes, you had to do those horrible things because you simply had no other choice.

Mrs. T was right. Of course she couldn't keep the baby. And, as she walked out the front door, a small bag of pizzelles to take with her, she tamped down the tiny, gnawing sense of doubt. What if her *little situation* was really a *little person* who was depending on her? What if *no other choice* was really shorthand for *no easy choice*? But she turned, forced a smile, and waved good-bye to Mrs. T.

It was no use, putting off the decision any longer.

No matter how she might feel, she simply couldn't keep the baby.

She had no other choice.

Chapter Nine

Heartbeat

Hattie turned the pamphlet over and over in her hands, clutching the now well-worn brochure as a kind of talisman: *What to Do When You're Pregnant* by Managed Motherhood. *Spoiler alert: we want you to have an abortion. It's easy, it's cheap, and you won't feel a thing.*

It felt beyond strange to be sitting in the same dingy waiting room, hearing the same muffled chanting through the walls, now as a patient of MM instead of an employee. And walking through the demonstrators on her way in—well, she was probably the only pregnant woman who hadn't been shouted at since they were accustomed to seeing her walk in the door each day as an employee. They ignored her—she was part of the other side—but they had no idea.

No idea she was pregnant.

And who could blame them? She fought back a bitter laugh; until recently, she hadn't had any idea either. She bowed her head, pretending to study the brochure some more so as not to meet Sally-Anne's sympathetic gaze any longer.

What you should know about in-clinic abortion. Hattie swallowed. If she'd read the pamphlet once, she'd read it a hundred times. *It uses suction to remove the pregnancy from your uterus.* Remove the pregnancy? What, like no one could just come out and say the truth about what was inside her? She didn't have a "pregnancy" inside her; it was a baby.

Or was it?

She'd never heard a happily pregnant mother refer to what was inside of her as anything but a *baby*. And it wasn't like anyone ever corrected a pregnant woman when she said she was having a baby. They wouldn't say, *No, you're actually having a pregnancy.*

She looked down at the pamphlet again, fighting the urge to rest her hand on her midsection. But this was calling what was inside her, what she had created, what was moving and growing right in her womb, a *pregnancy*. She remembered a training session, taught by Matilda, not long after she had begun working at MM.

Matilda had waggled a long purple fingernail, very insistent. "*Never use the word abortion, and never, ever use the word baby. It's just too painful and upsetting— too much emotional trauma—and we don't want that for our patients.*"

She had quickly learned the many euphemisms used every day at MM:

Terminate the pregnancy.

Products of conception.

Pregnancy tissue.

And now this: *remove the pregnancy*.

What if she were to change her mind and say that she wanted to keep the baby—um, the *pregnancy*? Would the *pregnancy* suddenly turn into a *baby*? Would it then become appropriate to be concerned about the baby's health and schedule a prenatal checkup?

Hattie sighed, tightly clutching the pamphlet as if to unlock some secret code that would reveal that the choice she was making was the right one. She didn't want to be coddled, the truth hidden from her behind innocuous phrases. She wasn't a woman that needed protection from making big decisions about hard truths. If she was the woman and she was making the choice about *her body*, then she didn't need some carefully manufactured phrases from the marketing department of some probably male-dominated corporation that was trying to tell her what to do with her baby—um, her pregnancy.

No. Hattie frowned. *You know what?*

My baby.

Because babies are babies whether they're inside or out.

Because babies are babies whether they're wanted or not.

And what, she was just going to get rid of it? What kind of mom did that make her? She fought back a shudder but then steeled her shoulders. The decision had already been made. It was the only decision that made any sense, and she was the one making the decision; no one else was making the decision for her, clever marketing puffery notwithstanding.

And yet she could feel her earlier resolve slipping away, and it gave her a sense of being unmoored. She felt as if she were slowly unwinding, cast adrift on a sea of uncertainty, and leaving behind all that she had dreamed for her life, all that her grandfather had wanted for her life. But why? Why did she have to feel like this? If all she wanted was to make her own way in the world and have the independence and freedom to make her own choices, why was she feeling so guilty?

She had taken her time over the last few weeks to think it over, to talk with Matilda, Mrs. T, even Sally-Anne who was now silent for a change, busying herself with paperwork behind the counter, wanting to give her some space. Hattie had spent her days floating through her work assignments, as in a trance, seeming to skim lightly along the earth's surface, in denial of what was happening inside her.

The protestors outside each day had not helped. One sign depicted the Liberty Bell with its famous inscription: *Proclaim LIBERTY Throughout All the Land unto ALL the Inhabitants Thereof* adjacent to an ultrasound image of a baby in the womb with the caption, *What about them?*

She tried not to think about a sign she had seen just this morning, as if crafted especially for her: *A baby's heart begins to beat between 18 and 25 days after conception.* The woman holding the sign, an old crone with wild eyes and frizzy hair, had even dared to catch her eye and shake the sign at her, as if adding an exclamation point to her message. Hattie had hurried inside, the encounter shaking her more than she wanted to admit. She was not a believer in signs—neither of the supernatural variety nor of the literal picketing variety, and certainly not omens—but everyone else had ignored her. Except for that old lady. Had she sensed something about her, known she was pregnant with some kind of elderly, witchy intuition?

Because—she counted in her head back to the day it had happened with *him*—it had been just over twenty-five days since he had taken what he wanted and left. The veneer of love slicked away to reveal the rotten core of lust within.

Twenty-five days, the outer edge of when the baby's heart—oh, the *pregnancy's heart*—first began to beat and sometimes as early as eighteen days. She knew it was true, too. She had done her research over the last few weeks. And she'd had no shortage of reading material.

She looked around the waiting room. She was coming to realize that most of the MM propaganda tended to downplay what was really happening inside her—ironic, given all the fancy equipment she had been learning about at the same time: high-def ultrasounds and sonograms that could display babies—um, *pregnancies*—with tiny hands and tiny feet, even fingers and toes, in 4-D, and even sophisticated Doppler measurements that could broadcast the baby's heartbeat on speakers clear as a bell, all measured by the TED units, of course. Not that most patients ending up seeing, or even wanting to see, those ultrasound images and sounds. Patients didn't come to MM to forge a closer connection with their baby but to dispense of an inconvenience.

Hattie licked her dry, chapped lips, trying not to think of her own lack of parental involvement and wishing the nurse would hurry up and fetch her out of this depressing prison cell of a waiting room before the walls closed in on her. She just wanted to get it over and done with, and then maybe she could stop thinking so much about heartbeats and legs and arms. And tiny footprints, those little toes, why—she scrunched her eyes shut tight, willing the train of thought to stop. And then, as if in response to her wish, the door opened, and Hattie opened her eyes, wild and shiny for a moment before she blinked rapidly, focusing in on the mop of dark, curly hair that poked around the doorframe.

Looking down at her phone and then up again, she called out, "Hattie? Hattie Martins?" Catching her eye, she smiled, tenderness mixed with impatience. "You can come back now."

Hattie recognized the nurse; Rosie was her name, although she didn't know her well. Both Matilda and Hattie had agreed that it would be best if it was someone Hattie did not know on a personal level.

Hattie stood up, leaving the brochure on the chair. Maybe someone else could make better use of it. For a moment, she imagined turning on her heel and running straight out the front door, never to return. But all she did was smile weakly at Sally-Anne and shuffle her scuffed sneakers toward Rosie, saying quietly, "I'm coming."

Ever since the decision, something inside her had felt strange, different, and it wasn't just the pregnancy. Only as she walked through the door, tuning out Rosie's murmured instructions, did she finally put a finger on it. Her heart sank. Her grandfather had been a strong, active, man's-man type of guy his entire life, all the way up until the sickness came, but he had gone out of his way to build up Hattie's self-worth, assuring her of her value as a girl and then a woman, even in this broken and infuriatingly depressing "man's world." She realized now that he was kind of an "OG feminist" in that funny, overbearing way of his, and more importantly, this was a big part of her ability to stand up for herself. An image of her refusing to back down from Mr. Green Eyes in the bad part of town flashed across her mind. Now, where had that thought come from? Maybe it was her heightened emotions dredging up all the memories. But what about now? What would her grandfather say about *this* decision?

Wasn't it the ultimate betrayal of feminism to let this man's world tell her that what was inside her— her child, maybe her daughter—wasn't important? That what was happening inside her wasn't all that big of a deal, that they would be happy to just "remove the pregnancy"? She wanted to scream out, but she just kept walking, her feet carrying her noiselessly and as of their own accord to the Medical

Ring. How could she ever say she was standing for women everywhere when she was refusing to stand for the little one inside her?

"Well, we're here." Rosie pushed open the door. "This is the Medical Ring, as you know." She gave a small smile. "So, you know the drill. We'll get you comfortable inside of your TED, and then it will be over shortly."

Hattie nodded, looking around the room as an excuse not to meet Rosie's eyes.

"Any questions?"

Hattie froze, feeling a stuffy, roaring sound in her ears, as if the room was slowly pressing in on her.

"Hattie?" Rosie frowned. "Do you have any questions for me?"

Blinking, Hattie shook her head.

"Okay, please follow me to Station 8." Rosie set off briskly, her shoes squeaking against the polished floors. "We'll get you all settled in, maybe with a nice beach experience, and get you nice and calmed down."

When they arrived at Station 8, Rosie tapped her phone to retract the TED's exterior, and before she could say a word, Hattie stepped neatly around her and into the TED, lying back against the deflated cushions with her eyes closed.

Rosie faltered. "Oh, okay. Right, you know exactly what to do already. So, if you're ready and don't have any questions—"

Hattie shook her head again, the leathery cushions crackling her hair with static.

"Okay, good. Then, this will only be a few minutes, and then you'll be all better. Okay, just cuing up your beach scene, and then you'll be all set." Hattie heard the sound of tapping while Rosie murmured under her breath. There was a light whirring sound and the exterior began to enclose around her again. "See you in a few."

Hattie felt the cushions begin to expand and press inward, and she gave her body over to its insistent demands, yielding to what was best, what was smart, what society said was her rightful choice.

She could hear the sounds of paradise around her, the gentle crashing waves of the beach as they rose and fell, rose and fell. A bird cried out with a screech, but her eyes remain closed. Long, spidery rivulets of silent tears snaked down the corner of each eye and traced across her cheeks, catching on her chin before falling as wet, salty droplets onto the interior of the TED.

And then it was over.

There were instructions, more pamphlets. Rosie insisted that she take the post-procedure pamphlets, as if those glossy, airbrushed stock photos with their boilerplate optimism would be enough to salve any lingering guilt over what used to pass for a trusted doctor-patient relationship. And then Hattie was outside, by herself. She'd learned that they send the post-procedure patients out a side door to avoid the crowds out front. But all the trite truisms from all the pamphlets in the world couldn't undo what she had done. Listlessly, she walked forward, dropping the fistful of brochures and other paperwork directly into a sloppy, overflowing trash can that smelled of sewage. She'd had a real, live baby inside her, depending on her, trusting her, and now, the baby was gone.

Gone.

Just like her grandfather.

All because of her.

Chapter Ten

Gen 6

She was supposed to be at work two hours ago, and yet here she lay, still in bed, flat on her back, eyes open but unseeing. She couldn't go back; she just couldn't. Not back *there*. Not after *what she'd done.*

Her phone had buzzed a dozen times—half of them displaying MM's main line, the other half Sally-Anne's personal number. She still hadn't bothered to move. Over the past week, she'd cried out her entire reservoir of tears, every pang and twitch of her aching body a reminder of what she'd done, of what was missing. *Who was missing.* Her baby.

A bitter laugh twisted her face. But she still had her dreams, her freedom, her independence—that made it all worth it, right? She should feel relieved. Now, she had her entire life before her and nothing or no one to hold her back. But why did she feel as if she'd betrayed some very important part of herself?

And the worst part—she cursed her inside knowledge of the TED units—before she was hustled away, right after the "pregnancy" was removed, she had glanced at the corner of Nurse Rosie's phone, just a quick one at the corner of the screen, but enough to see the capital F.

F for female.

She closed her eyes again slowly, willing herself to just sink through the bed, through the floor, down into the earth, through the crust and into the molten core to be subsumed, gone forever, along with all her poor, selfish decisions. She thought that a little bit of regret post-procedure would be a matter of course; it was only a natural part of things, what Matilda and Rosie and everyone had prepared her for—even those little brochures in their trite, superficial way had helped her with that—but the sharp, slicing pangs that clenched her insides, threatening to pull her under, those had started at seeing that little letter and hadn't let up, now over a week later. It wasn't supposed to be this bad, was it?

Because she'd had a girl. She'd been pregnant with a baby girl. Somehow, knowing this made everything more real and much, much worse. Though she knew she didn't deserve naming privileges, she couldn't help but think of her as a Jane, like her grandmother. Someone Hattie knew only from faded, foggy memories, but someone her grandfather had talked about ceaselessly and rapturously up until his final days. In fact, he had called out to her just moments before he passed. The scene was enough to either cure or ruin Hattie's love life forever; she still hadn't decided.

She counted the water stains on her ceiling once again, knowing that letting her mind circle around in endless loops was not healthy. She needed to go to work, find something to keep herself busy, throw herself into her job of caring for others at MM. A harsh laugh escaped her lips. Well, not anymore. She'd been given a week off of work to recover. But, now, today was supposed to be her first day back, and here she was, unable to move. Her job was probably gone about an hour and fifty-nine minutes ago when she hadn't clocked in.

Her eyes slowly closed. If only she could just fall back asleep, never to awake. If only—

A knock on her door, just feet away in the small one-bedroom apartment, flipped her eyes open. Who could that possibly be? She had friends, of course, but not the kind that just dropped by to hang out at 10:03 a.m. on a Monday, and if they were going to hang out, it certainly wouldn't be in her dump of an apartment, so tiny that it was practically the size of a closet. And her neighbors, well, everyone around here tended to keep to themselves, so—

Another knock, more insistent this time.

She jolted upright, leaning back on her elbows and debating if she could bring herself to get out of bed and answer the door. Robbers didn't knock first, did they? Not like she had anything worth stealing. If it was a burglar, he was pretty horrible at choosing his targets. Maybe, if she just stayed motionless, they would go away—

"Hattie? I know you're in there." The voice was clear through the thin door. "It's me, Sally-Anne." There was a pause. "From work."

Hattie fought back a groan. She would rather it be a gang of thieves. She liked Sally-Anne, but the last thing she wanted to think about was MM. Why couldn't they just let her be, let her move on?

"Come on, Hattie. I know you're in there." She heard rustling. "I brought some cronuts. Charles brought them in, of course. He misses you, Matilda misses you, I miss you, we all do." She paused a few moments. "Come on, Hattie. I walked all the way here on my break. Just let me in."

Groaning inside, she swung her legs around the side of her bed and slowly stood upright. "I'm coming," Hattie said softly.

Before she could hardly get the door open, Sally-Anne pushed through, wrapping her in an enormous bear hug, the paper bag of cronuts crinkling behind Hattie's back. A well of emotion at the unexpected gesture surged through Hattie, and she allowed her body to unstiffen and relax into the warm, prolonged embrace. Sally-Anne didn't say a word, but after a moment, she gave a gentle squeeze and released Hattie.

"So, um, thanks for coming, but if you're trying to talk me into—"

"Nice bedhead," Sally-Anne interrupted with a smile. She lifted the bag of cronuts. "Let's go sit and eat while we talk. Aren't you going to let me in?" Not even looking at her anymore, Sally-Anne had spotted the flimsy, paint-flecked card table and two folding chairs that served as one-third of Hattie's furnishings and was already spreading out the sugar-crusted pastries on a layer of napkins. "I'm starving; I had to fight off everyone else from eating them all, and I saved these last six for us, but I haven't even had one yet."

"Six?" Hattie raised an eyebrow, shocked into letting a tiny smile slip. "How bad exactly did you think I was? On my deathbed?"

"One cronut gets me through each workday, two are for days when corporate shows up, and three—" She let out a long, slow breath. "Well, three cronuts are for emergencies." She looked at Hattie, her eyes softening. "For those days when you just need a friend."

Hattie tipped her head, nodding thankfully. "Thanks, Sally-Anne. You didn't have to come all the way—"

"I know; I know." She smiled brightly. "But I wanted to."

"Well, thank you."

"Now, sit!" Sally-Anne extended a hand. "Let's eat."

"Okay." Pulling her seat back, Hattie felt a twinge of pain in her abdomen, reminding her all over again of what Sally-Anne had managed to make her forget over the last two minutes. She eased herself back into the seat, a shadow passing over her face.

"So," Sally-Anne said quietly, stuffing the final crumbs of her first cronut in and eyeing the second one hungrily, "you didn't come in to work today." She spoke matter-of-factly, licking her fingers precisely and sucking each fingertip with a resounding pop-pop-pop. The twin sparrow tattoos on each forearm appeared to bounce and hover in the air, intent on a bite for themselves but ever just out of reach. "Maybe you forgot today was the day you started back again, maybe the pain meds are making you feel a little out of it, maybe—"

"No." Hattie shook her head, nibbling delicately at first and then, discovering she was famished, giving in to Sally-Anne's example and wolfing her first cronut down as well. "I just didn't want to. I decided I'm not—"

"Uh-uh," Sally-Anne said, waggling a sugar-flecked finger. "*Maybe* you just called in to me this morning at the front desk to tell me you're still recovering and you'll be in in a few days or maybe even next week."

Hattie frowned. "But—"

"And *maybe* I just forgot to mention your call to Matilda because I got swamped, but then I remembered and felt bad, so I rushed over here to check in on you, and I'll head right back after eating my third cronut"—she nodded appreciatively at number three, already in her hand—"to tell Matilda you'll be in next Monday."

"I don't know…"

"Come on, Hattie." She lifted both eyebrows, cocking her head with an impudent flop of greasy blonde hair that set the hoops in her ears to jangling.

"You know you aren't going to find anything better for work, not around here."

She did have a point. Hattie shook her head. "But—"

Sally-Anne lifted a hand, chewing the last bite of number three. "Don't give me an answer. Because I'm leaving right now, and that's what I'm telling Matilda." Her gaze softened. "Just think about it until next Monday, okay? Just relax, get all better. I know it's not easy. I—" Her friendly face grew cold, hard; something flashed through her eyes, making her features seem sharper and more angular. "I know from *firsthand* experience." She looked at Hattie meaningfully. "It's not easy; I know."

An understanding passed between them: pain, their mutual companion; and hopes, dreams, and longing, their shared mirage. At last, Hattie nodded.

"And listen"—Sally-Anne's features grew tortured, her mouth screwed up, the debate whether or not to speak clearly evident—"I shouldn't say anything, but, well ..." She let out a long sigh, and her mouth turned into a thin, hard line. "But I'm going to anyway because, well, I just wish someone had done the same for me." Her voice trailed off.

Hattie frowned, feeling her body stiffen. "What are you saying?"

The blues of Sally-Anne's eyes seemed extraordinarily vivid and bright, like the sky behind a polar ice cap, and when she spoke, they were all Hattie could focus on, everything else falling away in a swirl of confusion. "I'm saying that you need to come back to work, so you can say good-bye."

The words came out like a whisper. "Say good-bye?"

"Something I never got the chance to do. It all happened so quick." Her blue eyes shone with intensity, made all the brighter because of the budding tears that sparkled and glistened, threatening to escape at any moment. "I don't ever talk about it"—she brushed the back of her hand against her cheek, turning the first escaped tear into a wet smear—"not until now, with you, but I think about it every day."

Hattie felt paralyzed, as if she were still in bed and trapped in a dream. "But I don't understand. How—"

"I don't want you to end up like me."

For the first time, Hattie got a fuller picture of how Sally-Anne felt. How long had she felt like this? And was this all Hattie had to look forward to?

Hattie's brow scrunched up. "Please. What do you mean? I don't—"

"Your baby's still alive."

The room seemed to tilt and spin. Hattie felt herself tipping to one side; whether that was in her imagination or actually happening, she wasn't sure. She fell back roughly in her chair, some part of her brain telling her she should attempt to pinch herself while the other part struggled mightily just to form a coherent sentence. "That's not funny. You should know that of—"

"I'm not joking," Sally-Anne said without a hint of a smile, her features flat and humorless. "We don't really talk about it publicly—only internally, of course—because we don't want mothers having second thoughts and coming back to us, but it's been part of our SOP, Standard-Operating-Procedure, ever since our Gen 6 TEDs, and that was years and years ago, from what I was told."

Hattie's eyes opened wide and wonderingly, as bright and shiny as Sally-Anne's, as she thought suddenly back to Matilda's abstruse comments about the womb room. "Are you saying my baby's not—"

Sally-Anne held up a hand. "Let me be clear. For all intents and purposes, your baby is gone, okay?"

Hattie nodded slowly, not really understanding.

"The TEDs, a *long* time ago, stopped doing the D&C and D&E abortion techniques that the old human abortion doctors used to do back in the day—much too gruesome, and the rise of the Internet and high-def video and pictures made it a public relations disaster when any random person could just type into a search engine and see the body parts," she spoke slowly, her voice rote and distant, as if reciting facts while forcing herself to be an impartial observer. "Now, the TEDs almost exclusively use the suction technique and very early in pregnancy, so the bodies are small enough to be sucked out intact and all in one piece—at least, most of the time—and with very little laminaria." At this, Sally-Anne laughed bitterly. "Funny in a twisted kind of way, how far we've come with abortion technology so that machines do practically everything, and yet we still use seaweed for dilation."

"But"—Hattie blinked, trying to get Sally-Anne back on track—"you're saying the TEDs *take the baby out intact* and then *the baby stays alive?*"

"Yes, sometimes for months, I think. The TED doesn't even take the baby through the birth canal and out the cervix until it sucks it right into an artificial womb." She inclined her head. "It's really pretty amazing. Some genius scientist a long time ago invented an artificial womb. You heard about that, I'm sure?"

Hattie nodded slowly. She hated watching the news, but she thought she remembered her grandfather mention something about it a long time ago.

"Anyway, the baby doesn't even leave the mother's body until it's in the new womb."

"That sounds—"

"Ridiculous? Far-fetched?" Sally-Anne shrugged. "Maybe, maybe not. You've seen what the TEDs can do. Matilda explained it to me like those old tools a roadside mechanic would use to get into your vehicle when you locked your keys in the car—you know, the ones with the inflatable rubber balloon on the end of a large stick?"

Hattie nodded. She's never had a car, let alone locked her keys out of one, but she'd seen enough old TV shows to be familiar with how the tool might work.

"You jam it in the crevice of the doorframe and then pump away until the balloon expands. It's tough rubber, you know, and then you've got a wide opening to get the lock open. Same concept here, except the rubber-like inflatable balloon is the artificial womb. It's actually made of a composite of that laminaria seaweed stuff, so it just seals the baby up and then pulls it out, totally intact and with everything it needs to survive right inside the balloon womb."

Hattie grimaced, the pain in her abdomen seeming to intensify at the thought.

"I know; I know. I'm sorry." Sally-Anne lifted her chin. "But we're both medical professionals, right? And, if we're both going to be nurses together someday…"

"You've been studying," Hattie said weakly, too stunned to even form another rational sentence.

"Yep," Sally-Anne said, clearly proud. "I ask a lot of questions and explore around MM, talk to people, and I read everything, even all the manuals in our archive library on our phones."

"Matilda explained this to you?" Hattie questioned, trying not to let any hint of disbelief creep into her voice.

"I'm not making this up!" Sally-Anne's face grew pink. "It's not exactly something MM publicizes, especially after that *harvesting body parts and then selling them* scandal a long time ago. You can look it all up. For a while, the MM focus-grouped a big marketing campaign that played up this new *humane* abortion procedure. *We don't harvest baby parts—at least, not right away! We do this new safe, humane procedure!* Blah, blah. But …"

"But what?" Hattie quickly countered.

Sally-Anne shrugged. "Well, they quickly discovered that people would rather just not know the details."

Hattie felt a sinking sensation in the pit of her stomach, but she couldn't stop herself from speaking. "They just want to be rid of their problem."

Sally-Anne nodded, her voice barely audible. "Yes."

Hattie swallowed, her throat suddenly feeling dry and grainy, and felt a strange sense of knowing what was coming next. "So, what do they do with the babies after they're put in the artificial wombs?"

Sally-Anne frowned. "I don't really know. They stay on-site for a little while, in storage, before they're trucked away. I know because I sign the deliveryman in every couple weeks, and he's memorable, to say the least—"

"Where are they stored?" Hattie asked, annoyed at Sally-Anne for thinking now was the time to talk about some cute delivery guy. She took a deep breath. "The womb room?"

Sally-Anne's eyes widened. "You know about—"

"No," Hattie said flatly. "I mean, not really. I just heard the name."

Sally-Anne nodded. "Okay, I didn't think so. So, you've never been there. It's not really a secret or anything, but it's all under heavy lock and key. I've only seen in there once, and it's kind of creepy, to be honest. But I can take you to the door, and then you could—" She paused, lowering her voice, as if suddenly remembering they weren't just talking one health professional to the next but about Hattie's baby. "And then you could say good-bye, if you want." She ducked her head, her voice tiny. "Get some closure maybe."

"Yes," Hattie spoke softly, her voice sounding far away, as if it were coming from someone else. "Yes, I'd like that. You're right; I'll come back to work."

"Okay"—Sally-Anne raised her eyebrows in shock and then reached down to hug Hattie—"that's great. That's great, Hattie. I'm so glad."

Her voice muffled by Sally-Anne's hair, Hattie robotically patted Sally-Anne's back as she spoke, "Not Monday though. Tomorrow. Tell Matilda I'll be back in to work tomorrow."

"Oh, okay. Well then"—withdrawing her embrace and holding Hattie's shoulders at arm's length, Sally-Anne paused before smiling again— "that's great. I will. Now, I'd better get going. I need to hurry back."

Another hug, and then Sally-Anne was gone, leaving nothing but the crumpled paper bag behind her.

Hattie sat motionless in her seat, realizing that, for the first time in over two years, someone had sat in her grandfather's chair. Templing her fingers, she slowly leaned her head forward until her elbows collapsed, followed by her entire upper body, hugging against the card table full of so many memories, and then she wept.

Chapter Eleven

It Hurts

I moan, feeling myself come to. My eyelids flutter open and then close again as if glued shut.

He was right. It hurts.

With herculean effort, I pull myself upright, confused by the restraining pressure on my lap until I realize it's the seat belt, maybe more useful in my current state of disorientation than expected. I remember his face, so somber at my insistence on pushing the button, and think that maybe I should have listened to him.

No.

I struggle to open my eyes again.

It's always better to know.

"Shh, there now." I feel a warm hand lightly brushing a wisp of hair across my forehead. "It doesn't seem like it now, but it's going to be okay."

It's him. His voice is strong, but I sense a hitch, as if he's been crying. The oddest thought pops into my head. *Maybe my pain hurts him just as much as it does me. Maybe even more.* His hand is uncommonly warm to the touch, but it feels good on my forehead.

I wish he wouldn't stop, but something in his low murmur of encouragement seems to be readying me, preparing me, for something. He doesn't have to say it; I know I have to go back.

Still, I haven't been able to open my eyes fully, but already, I feel myself slipping back, down under. Back to where I came from, the place with all the pain.

"You'll be back," he says, reassuring me.

It's the last thing I hear before all is black again.

Chapter Twelve

The Kick

It was to be at break time; that was what they'd decided. Their first break of the day, usually around ten, was ideal because both Hattie and Sally-Anne would have someone to cover for them—Sally-Anne from the front desk and Hattie from routine cleanup, not yet allowed back in the Medical Ring on her first day back.

And the most important thing: every day, Matilda would stroll out to the waiting room area. "Just getting the lay of the land," was how she'd put it.

But everyone knew she timed her check-ins to coincide with Charles's entrance from doing patient escort service out front, his scheduled break time being nine thirty a.m. sharp. Then, after some playful banter and flirting, Charles would saunter back to the break room or the restroom, and Matilda would high-step it back to her office, plowing through paperwork at an incredible speed, the sound of her whistling heard down the hall. Sally-Anne had said it was a standing joke among the receptionists that the hour following Charles's appearance was when Matilda got the other seven hours' worth of work done.

Hattie looked at the clock on the wall, forcing a bored expression on her face, though she felt as if her heartbeat could be seen thumping through her scrubs.

9:58.

Close enough.

She forced herself to calmly finish unloading the final carton of bandages, carefully stacking them on the bottom shelf in the supply closet. Still the new kid on the block, she ended up with all the thankless and menial tasks, but she understood that was just the way it was. With a slight wince—she still didn't feel one hundred percent—she rose to her feet and stood with her hand leaning against the doorframe for support. It seemed kind of ridiculous and borderline insane, this *plan* of theirs, but Sally-Anne seemed to think it was important that Hattie go. And, despite her forced restraint, there was a reckless hope that dared to dart like a kite caught in a sudden updraft inside her; she felt herself drawn to the room.

The room with her baby.

Her *still very much alive* baby.

She was under no illusions about what would happen. It wasn't like she could just bust her way in and jam the baby back in; that decision had been made last week, which already seemed like ages ago.

And, besides, even if it were a possible thing, what kind of mom aborts her baby *and then wants it back*? She swallowed. Not a good one; she knew that.

Or maybe just a regular mom, a flawed one, a real one, something inside of her said.

What kind of mom hadn't ever felt overwhelmed, wanting to give up and just call it quits? Maybe that meant she was just a normal human being.

She held her eyes shut for a moment, attempting to squeeze out the swirling, whirling, unwelcome intrusion of thoughts. Opening her eyes, she looked at the clock.

10:01.

Steeling her resolve, she stepped out into the hall and toward Sally-Anne's desk.

"Oh, hey, Hattie! Ready for break time?" Sally-Anne's voice rang out, bright and artificial. A natural in the acting department she was not. She stood up from her desk suddenly, stretching an arm out woodenly and pointing to her chair as she looked to one of the other girls in the office. "Can you cover for me? Hattie and I are going on break."

As the other girl, Bettina, gave a bored nod, Sally-Anne turned to Hattie and had the audacity to wink, eyes shining brightly.

Pursing her lips and trying to fight back the groan that wanted to escape them, Hattie took a deep breath. "Well, let's go," she responded, holding the door open for Sally-Anne.

After a few minutes of walking down corridor upon endless corridor, turning left and then right and then left again, badging in with Sally-Anne's badge to go from one zone to another—she had access to a surprising amount of the building since she often escorted delivery people back to any number of destinations within the maze of long hallways and locked rooms—they were suddenly at the end of a nondescript corridor and standing in front of an unmarked door. Abruptly, Sally-Anne stopped talking, though she had chattered nervously the entire way.

Hattie swallowed, wanting to look away, maybe even turn and run, but she was unable to keep her eyes from fixating on a rectangular glass window in the top third of the door. The room appeared to be nothing but darkness and shadows within.

Finally, Sally-Anne spoke, this time having the good grace to speak softly, "This is it." She tucked a strand of stringy yellow hair behind one ear, eyes intent on Hattie. "This is where they keep the babies in the artificial wombs." She lifted her badge slowly, extending it from the cord that attached it to her hip. "This will get you in." She paused, her face now serious as she considered Hattie. Her voice was unusually quiet. "Are you sure? You don't have to, you know. I kind of pressured you just because I thought that was what I would've want—"

"I'm sure," Hattie interrupted, not taking her eyes off the door. "Badge me in. How much time do we have?"

Sally-Anne glanced down at her phone and then back up again. "Five minutes." She shifted her stance, nervously glancing down the hallway. "I'll stand out here and keep watch."

Quickly, before she could lose her nerve, Hattie nodded. "I'm ready. Do it."

When Sally-Anne extended her card, the door pinged, a small green light near the handle coming to life. Pulling the door open, Hattie took a deep breath and stepped across the threshold.

Blinding white lights flicked on instantaneously, and she bit back a cry.

Just motion detecting lights, she told herself as she breathed in and out, willing her skyrocketing heart rate to slow.

Many of the rooms in the building were like that, run by a timer that would power the lights on when sensing movement and off after a period of inactivity.

Steeling her resolve, she walked forward briskly, swiveling her head to get her own "lay of the land." It was clean, bright, industrial. Rows and rows of expensive-looking minimalist equipment hummed and pulsed with quiet electronic energy. This room looked even more like a server farm than some of the other places she had been in the Medical Ring. A very hygienic server farm, that was. The room reeked of an antiseptic, ammonia-like smell that felt harsh against her nostrils. She hoped the babies weren't taking in any of the fumes, though knew the artificial wombs had to be ultra-protected and enclosed against anything in the external environment—or at least, they should be—though little did she know.

Her pace slowed. So, where were they? Where were the babies? Were they even in the right place? A sudden jolt of fear flooded her brain. Maybe they had all been taken away; maybe they were too late. Maybe they—

She pivoted on her heel, looking up and noticing for the first time a small graphical display on the shell of each exterior unit. Patient numbers. Her heart began to pound. She knew her number.

She walked quickly, her gaze panning over the displays rapidly now that she knew what to look for, and then she stopped. This was it: row five, the very first unit. She took a deep breath and stepped into the aisle before she could lose her nerve.

The soles of her shoes squeaked against the linoleum as she pulled to a stop, her hand drifting to her mouth. At the end of the rows, where she had entered the room, there had been minimal visibility into the server-like storage racks that towered at least twice as high as Hattie and paneled with some type of fiberglass exterior. But now, walking down the rows and looking in from the side view, she could clearly see what they housed.

Babies.

Dozens and dozens—no, hundreds, maybe even thousands of them, and—this part made sense yet somehow totally caught her by surprise—they were perfectly visible. For some reason, Sally-Anne's description of the inflating carjack balloon had caused her to envision the babies enclosed within an artificial womb that kept them hidden from view. But this was definitely not the case; each artificial womb hung from a mass of tubing, like a swollen rain droplet, the exterior shining and shimmering like an amniotic sac—which, Hattie realized with a start, it probably was.

Of course, she thought. The smartest way to keep the baby alive outside of the mother was simply to take the womb with it; the babies *were still in their amniotic sacs*, and now, they hung suspended and constrained by some kind of fibrous mesh material that enclosed and strengthened the sac.

And—she reached a tentative hand out, her fingertips shaking—the amniotic sac was entirely translucent, revealing a tiny human form slowly swirling and rotating in the amniotic fluid, tiny arms and legs, even fingers and toes clearly visible. And this—right here in front of her—this was *her* womb with *her* baby in it. She blinked rapidly.

Well, not her baby anymore. She tried to think of it as just a collection of body parts. Not as Jane, like her grandmother, but seeing all the little appendages actually made it even more difficult. Suddenly, it was as if she could hear the protestors' chants from outside: *Not your body, not your body, not your body.* Her fingertip made contact with the sac, the gentlest of touches, and the sac, sticky to the touch, depressed, feeling like a plasticky, more resilient version of a bubble.

With a half-roll and twirl, the baby twisted sideways, kicking its heel out faster than Hattie thought possible and making contact with her finger.

Jerking her finger back as if she'd touched a hot iron, she screamed, a bloodcurdling wail that seemed to come from some closed-off, hidden part of her that she didn't like to acknowledge was there, pulled out of the dark and brought suddenly into the light. Stumbling backward, her shoulders shaking, she brushed against the row behind her and then twisted violently away in surprise. Sobbing uncontrollably, she pitched forward, careening back to the door.

The door flung open, and Sally-Anne's concerned face poked through. "Hattie! What is it?" Her voice hissed down the aisle, the whisper carrying and echoing in the large room. "What's wrong? What happened?"

Her eyes wild, Hattie flung herself against Sally-Anne's chest. "Let's go; let's go. We have to get out of here." Her feet kept churning, propelling Sally-Anne back even as she continued to backpedal, a confused look on her face. Hattie's voice cracked. "Please, just take me back. Now, let's go. We have to go. I can't be in there anymore."

"Okay, okay. Come on, this way."

Hattie felt Sally-Anne's concerned gaze on her as they walked down the hallway side by side, their steps quickening, but she didn't say a word. Hattie's mind roiled; it was one thing to dismiss what was inside of you as being inconsequential, a clump of cells, a mass. Even the properly-scientific term *fetus* had come to represent non-human rather than just a human at a particular stage of development, like *toddler* or *adolescent* or *teenager.* This was all easy to do when you couldn't see anything, couldn't see what was really happening, but you couldn't exactly do the whole *out of sight, out of mind* routine when the fetus, the little human being, the little baby was moving around in a translucent womb with arms and legs and fingers and toes on full display. In her gut, she knew this was why MM had always discouraged ultrasounds and sonograms until the patient had already agreed to the abortion. And, even with all the remarkable and mind-boggling advances in technology like the TEDs, what she had seen of baby Jane seemed intentionally minimal: the images blurry, fuzzy, non-distinct, and described with euphemisms like "product of conception" or "uterine contents," all carefully designed to make her "removal of the pregnancy" seem like just another routine medical procedure.

But it wasn't just another medical procedure, and it wasn't just a blob of tissue. She stifled a sob; she had removed a baby from inside her, a tiny, living human being, one that depended on her, and one that was now all alone, without her mother, and hooked up to a sinister, blinking machine in a dark, forgotten room. And the worst part—she hadn't even had the courage to stay pregnant long enough to have the baby and give her up to someone else. She had just discarded her. When Jane needed her most, she had bailed, just like when she'd given up on her grandfather.

Her pace slowing, Sally-Anne looked over and spoke softly, hesitantly, "Are you okay? Want to run into the restroom for a minute?" She gestured to a door ahead. "I can wait outside."

"No, no, that's okay. I'm fine now," Hattie said, taking a deep breath and forcing a smile even as the lie turned sour on her lips.

Sally-Anne paused, her eyes narrowing slightly, before she nodded. "Okay, if you say so. What—"

She looked up and down the hall and then locked back on Hattie's eyes. "What did you see in there?"

"I saw babies," Hattie said simply. "Real, living human babies."

"Okay…"

Hattie closed her eyes and then opened them slowly, feeling as if a great heaviness pressed down, constricting her on all sides. Her mouth firmed into a hard line. "And I need to know what happens to them."

Sally-Anne sighed, letting out a long exhale. "I was afraid you'd say that." As if in slow motion, she reached into the pocket of her scrubs and extracted a small yellow sheet of paper. "I just had this feeling about you. And I might come to regret this, but—" Abruptly, she shoved the paper into Hattie's hands. "Here, take this."

Hattie turned the paper over in her hands, recognizing the MM logo instantly. "What is this?"

"It's a delivery order from MM corporate."

Hattie looked closer. "For *genetic material*? Is that—"

"Yes." Sally-Anne nodded. "What you just saw. At least I think so; that's the room I always take the delivery guy to whenever we get one of those."

Flipping the paper over and then back again, she frowned. "I don't see an address. Where do they take the, um, cargo after leaving here?"

"Not sure." Sally-Anne shrugged, taking the paper and slipping it back into her pocket. "Can't be too far though. The delivery guy, the cute one, he's local. It could even be here in Philly. We'd better get back."

She started walking and then paused, turning to Hattie. With a tiny voice, she asked, "Do you feel better now? Now that you've had some closure?"

"I-I'm not sure—"

"Because, Hattie…" The tone of Sally-Anne's voice dropped slightly. "It hurts to hear this—I know; trust me—but *your baby's gone*. You gave it up. There's no going back even if you wanted to." She exhaled, running fingers through her scraggly blonde hair. "I know what you saw in the room. They look like babies, sure, and they really do, but they're not viable outside the artificial womb, and they don't even know what's happening around them. They might each technically be a *human being*, but they aren't yet a *person*, you know? So, I know this is rough—" At this, she latched on to Hattie's arm, her eyes wide and pleading. "Please, you have to believe me; I *know* this firsthand. I know how much it hurts; I really do." Her grip on Hattie's forearm relaxed. "But we can't get all emotional. We are helping all these women who come in here." Her voice grew small. "We helped *you*. And, really, we're helping those babies, too. What kind of life would they eventually have had anyway?" She turned to resume walking.

Hattie followed, murmuring something unintelligible. Sally-Anne had a point, and Hattie didn't have an answer for her. What kind of life would her baby have had? Not a good one. Bitterly, Hattie hung her head. She could hardly even provide for herself, let alone a baby.

Sally-Anne's voice rose. "We did what we had to do, you and I, didn't we? It's not like we even really had a choice. And, besides, it's more like they were a potential life than a life anyway." Sally-Anne turned back and continued marching to the waiting room.

Hattie nodded vaguely, still too caught up in her emotions to trust herself to speak. A *potential life* and not a *life*? How could some single-celled organism on Mars be called a life and not a tiny human being with a beating heart? And how could a human being not be a person? How was that even possible? But those questions were academic; she knew that what would keep her up tonight would be something else entirely.

It hadn't even happened inside her; it was only for the briefest of moments, and it was the exact opposite of the stereotypical joyful circumstances that usually surrounded this milestone event. But all the same, something had kindled inside her, underneath the initial terror, maybe maternal instinct, maybe purely a biological response over which she had no control, but it had done something to her. It had affected her deeply.

She had felt the kick.

Chapter Thirteen

The Touch

I flinch back from the touch.

It's not that I don't like the feeling. Making contact just surprised me; that's all.

"There, there. It's okay. It's just me."

The voice sounds familiar, and I struggle to place it, but then it comes to me all in a rush. Oh, it's him. I'm back. It wasn't the-the touch from over *there*— the other place, the one with all the pain.

My eyes flutter open once again, and the first thing I see is his wide, concerned face hovering over me. His features relax into a smile, and he gently touches my shoulder. The touch is soft, full of love. It's nice.

"Hey," I say softly, my voice sounding more like a croak and strange to my ears. I clear my throat, and the volume improves. "I'm back." After stating the obvious, I swallow, noticing for the first time how dry and scratchy my throat feels. Seeing something in his face, I continue, "But—"

"But not for long."

I'm not sure what to say, so I just say, "Okay." An overwhelming sense of loss floods over me, and I'm not sure if I should be feeling this way because I have to leave *here* or because I know I can't stay *there* much longer.

He looks curiously at me. "Are you glad you did it? Glad you pushed the button?"

I try to concentrate, and I feel my face wrinkling into a deep frown. Surprisingly, I find that I'm kind of fuzzy on the actual details of what's been happening *over there*, but the feelings are still with me. Pain. Confusion. A moment of buoyant, heart-pounding joy punctuated by the free fall of despair, heartbreak, and loss. Right now, *here*, I feel loved, claimed, wanted, but I can still feel that echo of abandonment and loss from over there. I wonder if it's permanent; I know it's just a memory, this remnant of feeling I have. It can't belong here, but I still feel it all the same.

I snap to and notice he is still watching me, his face indicating he understands my thoughts. He extends a hand to my shoulder again, his touch like a whisper against my flesh. I don't shrink away this time.

"It's time," he says. "Are you ready?"

Will I ever be? I think. But I find myself nodding.

Before it even seems possible, I find myself slipping away, back under, my eyelids drooping and so heavy.

The last thing I remember is his touch, and then I'm gone.

Chapter Fourteen

Tuck and Run

"Psst, Hattie!"

Hattie jumped, banging her head on a shelf. Frowning, she turned around slowly, rubbing the top of her head that would probably turn into a knot by the end of the hour. "What is so important that you had to go sneaking up behind me like that?"

Sally-Anne inclined her head beyond the doorframe, a sheepish grin on her face. "Whoops, my bad. Well, anyway"—her eyes lit up—"I came to get you. It's break time."

Hattie shook her head, turning back to the shelves. "I can't. I—"

"Oh, no, no, no. Believe me." Sally-Anne brushed a strand of flaxen hair behind her ear and waggled her eyebrows suggestively. "You want to take your break *right now*; just trust me on this."

Standing up and rubbing the crick in her lower back, Hattie sighed. "And why is that exactly?"

"So…" Sally-Anne twirled the end of her hair— full of split-ends, Hattie noticed with annoyance— and practically purred, "Remember that cute guy I told you about?"

Rolling her eyes, Hattie groaned. "What? Seriously?"

"*The delivery guy*," Sally-Anne said meaningfully, tipping her chin down. "You know, who comes to pick up—"

"Oh, right," Hattie said quickly, her heart beginning to race like a car slipping into gear and then catching.

"Well, let's go!" Sally-Anne said brightly, spinning on her heel.

Wordlessly, Hattie followed her, maneuvering an unpacked industrial-sized box of adhesive bandages to a shelf as she left, letting the door swing shut behind her with a whoosh. On some level, she knew she was on a fool's errand; there was no outcome to this little quest of hers, to find out what happened to the babies in the artificial wombs, to find out what happened to *her* baby, wherein she could find herself feeling better about what she had done. And yet some small part of her still held out hope that Sally-Anne would be right. That maybe, if she could officially say good-bye, see this thing to the end, then she would have some measure of closure.

Sally-Anne's voice was bubbly up ahead, chattering away about this or that date she'd been on last weekend, but *those guys were losers, nothing compared to this guy*, the squeaking of her shoes the only punctuation that interrupted her rapid-fire gossip.

Hattie trailed slightly behind, her mind elsewhere, before she suddenly stopped and spoke, "Sally-Anne?"

She slowed to a stop, looking back over her shoulder slowly as if loathed to cease her monologue. "What, Hattie?"

"Why are you doing this?" Hattie asked quietly. "Why are you helping me? I know you don't think this is a good idea."

"Because," Sally-Anne spoke forcefully, "you're my friend." She shrugged, her face softening. "And I've been there. I know how it feels. I know you want answers; you want to make sense of it all, maybe feel like there's some good that will come out of a difficult situation. That's only natural. I felt the same way; believe me." She paused, shifting from one hip to the other and then locking into her eyes. "But, Hattie?"

Hattie swallowed, suddenly feeling short of breath. "Yeah?"

"Sometimes, there are no easy answers. We did what we had to do, each one of us. You know that, right?"

Not trusting herself to speak, Hattie nodded slowly.

"And it's fine to ask questions. I'm your friend, and believe me, I want to do all I can to help you get whatever you need to feel better, but..."

Uncharacteristically, Sally-Anne's features seemed to shrink and contort, a pinch of pain spasming across her face. Pulling herself together with what seemed to be great effort, she spoke in a lighthearted way, but her eyes were cold and serious, "Just look at me; I'm all messed up, and it's been years since I ... since I did it, so who knows? Maybe you shouldn't listen to a word I say." Her laugh was cold and mechanical, a raspy bark that set Hattie's teeth on edge. "Well, here we are." The cheerful mask was back on, and Sally-Anne nodded toward the door leading to the waiting room while raising an eyebrow. "Ready?"

Hattie nodded. As she would ever be.

As she elbowed the door open, an overjoyed smile blossomed across Sally-Anne's features, and she waved Hattie in. "Tucker, oh, Tucker. Ready to get signed in? I want you to meet someone. This is—"

Hattie stepped into the waiting room and froze.

Emerald eyes sparkled, widening in surprise before slanting and locking on Hattie like a panther. The smooth, confident voice drawled slowly, dripping like honey.

"Hey there, Hot Sauce."

Sally-Anne frowned, confusion wrinkling up her forehead and freezing the flirty, catty look on her face. "You-you guys know each other already?"

"We're acquainted," he said, his eyes never leaving Hattie.

Her mind raced, remembering all that she had said and done to him when they first met. Had she reacted too rashly with the stun gun? Self-defense or not, she didn't want to get *that* kind of reputation around the office. He could make trouble for her here at work if he wanted to.

He still hadn't blinked, an observation which Hattie thought was borderline sociopathic until she finally remembered to blink herself, catching her first breath in the process.

A broad grin broke out on his face, as if he had won some kind of contest, and his face relaxed slightly, now smiling and blinking at normal intervals.

"Somewhat, I should say. Somewhat acquainted." He stretched out a hand, a tiny smile playing on his features as he held himself with an overly professional bearing. "I'm Tuck." He shook her hand, his body stiff and rigid, as if he were a disinterested businessperson, but with a smirk. "Some people like to still call me Tucker though."

He shot a grin in Sally-Anne's direction, and she responded with an audible sigh of relief, returning his attention with a dazzling smile of her own.

"Hattie." She kept her voice neutral. "My name's Hattie." *Not Hot Sauce*, she bit back just in time.

He inclined his head slightly, that cocky grin never leaving his face. "A pleasure," he said in such a tone that Hattie wasn't sure on whose part he was referring. "Well ..." He turned his full attention to Sally-Anne, dismissing Hattie.

She resisted the urge to give in to playing his little games, keeping her face placid and uncaring, and yet, inwardly, she seethed.

He placed a hand on Sally-Anne's upper arm, his bicep rippling even through his shirtsleeve. Hattie noticed, but then she quickly focused back on Sally-Anne's face, a picture of ecstasy.

He withdrew his hand, clearing his throat. "I've got a requisition for two pickups today."

Bobbing her head from side to side, Sally-Anne pursed her lips, overselling the flirtation—in Hattie's unbiased opinion. "You got a delivery order for that?"

As if by magic, a tri-color sheaf of papers appeared, and he handed it over with a curt and matter-of-fact *the flirting phase is over* look on his face.

Seeming to intuit this immediately, Sally-Anne got down to business, too, accepting the papers and tipping them in Hattie's direction, so she could read the patient numbers. She breathed a sigh of relief when she didn't recognize her own. She gave a tiny head shake to Sally-Anne, who quickly signed the bottom, ripped off the top yellow copy, and then handed the rest back to him.

With a sniff, Sally-Anne inclined her head toward Hattie, her face expressionless. "Hattie can walk you back." She turned to walk back to her desk at reception. Hattie couldn't see her face, but she thought she detected a note of hurt in her voice. "Since you two are already so well *acquainted* with each other."

Taking a deep breath, Hattie kept her eyes on Sally-Anne's back, studiously ignoring the haughty gaze and wolfish grin of her supposed long-time acquaintance. "Let's go," she said softly.

"Right behind you," he intoned, his voice rumbling and full of barely suppressed humor.

As soon as they got through the door and Hattie found that they were alone in the hallway, she whirled around to face him. "We are *not* some kind of long-lost friends or anything, just *acquaintances*, in the loosest form of the word imaginable."

He raised an eyebrow, his green-eyed gaze frank and assessing. "Easy there, Hot Sauce. You gonna pull another prod on me? I'm just trying to do my job here."

She huffed, resisting the urge to punch him in the nose. He was just so infuriating. Regardless, she dipped her head slightly; it most certainly would be embarrassing if any of the other staff found out she had been wandering the streets, attacking people with stun guns. Her face blanched, and he seemed to pick up on her discomfort immediately, like a predator sensing weakness in his prey.

"So, is that how they teach you to handle difficult patients around here?" He ruefully rubbed the side of his neck, eyeing her meaningfully. "I think the hickey you gave me went away though."

"Will you stop it!" She glanced over her shoulder to make sure no one else was coming down the hallway. Though the walls in the Medical Ring were of sturdier construction, she knew from firsthand experience that the walls in this hall were paper-thin. She and Sally-Anne had made many a joke at the expense of Charles and Matilda's not-so-secret office romance. Thinking of Sally-Anne sitting at her desk and hearing their voices rise and fall just on the other side of the wall made Hattie's face blush with a rush of surprising intensity. "Let's go!" she hissed. "Come on, it's down here."

"Oh, I know the way." He extended a hand down the hall with a mock half-bow. "But, by all means, lead the way."

Stepping forward, Hattie murmured, "Oh, you, you've been here before."

"What? You thought just because I live in the hood, I didn't have a job?" His voice was airy, light, with a note of humor, but Hattie detected an undercurrent of resentment. "That it? Maybe you thought I just spent all day *on my porch* and never left that part of town?"

Hattie swallowed. So, he had remembered her comment.

His voice rose slightly, sounding strained. "Thought maybe I'd be familiar with this abortion clinic but only from dropping off all my *baby mamas* when I wanted to make a problem disappear, huh? That how you had me pegged?"

She slowed her pace, not sure what to say.

"Yeah," he snorted, shaking his head. "That's what I thought. Don't forget; when you come from a certain part of town, people still see what they want to see, no matter what type of job you have. Don't ever forget that."

"So," she spoke quickly and softly, deciding that this thin-walled hallway was not the place for *that* kind of discussion, "what exactly is your job?"

Pausing mid-stride, he looked hard at Hattie. Then, his features relaxed, and he snorted, laughing quietly. "Gonna play nice now, huh, Hot Sauce?"

She felt her face growing red. "I was just asking a simple question. Why do you have to make everything so difficult?"

"Okay, okay, truce," he said, holding up an open palm. He slid in front of her, blocking her forward progress down the hallway and causing her to come to an abrupt stop to keep from bouncing into his chest. "Let's start over." He extended a hand. "My name's Tuck."

"Hattie," she said after a pause, feeling silly and also very conscious of her pulse speeding up and making her feel slightly short of breath.

"Nice to meet you, Hattie." His grip was strong yet gentle. Her hand felt delicate and tiny, fragile like a bird's wing in comparison to his bear paw of a hand. Slowly, he released her. "What do you do around here, Hattie?"

"I'm a nursing aide." She found herself speaking as if by rote, unable to look away from his glittering green eyes. "I haven't been here very long. In fact, the day—" She paused, feeling foolish, but the words kept pouring out. "The day we first, um, met, when I was in such a hurry, well, that was my first day actually."

He seemed to find this news enormously funny, tilting his head back and roaring with laughter, his chest expanding and shaking with the riptides of amusement. "Aha-ha, your first day, was it?"

Her eyes grew wide, shocked at the sudden outburst. Strangely enough, an image of her grandfather cackling over a card game swooped in from nowhere, alighted softly along the edges of her consciousness, and then it was gone, taking her breath away in its wake. Closing her slack-jawed mouth, she frowned. "It's really not *that* funny, is it?"

Wiping a tear from his eye, he shook his head. "No, not really. I mean, kind of. You-you were intent on this career choice, huh?" His voice was mirthful, yet he gave her a wry look. "You were willing to tase anyone who got in your way, huh?"

She ducked her head, chagrined, and then looked up again quickly, wondering just how much of this conversation was being heard in rooms beyond this hallway.

"Whatever," she said softly. But she smiled. "Well, now that we've officially met, let's get going."

He remained standing, blocking her way, an impertinent smile on his face that quickly morphed into a look of annoyance. "Aren't you going to ask about me?"

"Oh." She stepped back, caught off guard. "Well, I already—I mean, you're just the delivery guy, right? You do deliveries?"

"*Just* the delivery guy? I *do deliveries?*" His perfectly lipped, wide mouth turned down at the corners. "Well, I do pick up and deliver items as part of my job, yes, but I am *not just* a delivery guy." He pulled himself upright, standing a little taller, his chest out, maybe without even noticing he was doing it. "I'm actually a lab tech for Progenitor. We're a wholly owned subsidiary of Managed Motherhood, by the way, although we like to stay behind the scenes for the most part. But we are essentially working for the same company." He lifted an eyebrow at Hattie.

"And, since you're a nursing aide, then that means I'm kind of like your boss."

Snorting, Hattie shook her head. "Please, you wish. And you wondered why I didn't ask what you—"

"Oh, hi, Tucker!" a voice called out behind Hattie.

Turning quickly, she saw Matilda striding up, a wide smile parting her dark red, heavily lipsticked lips to reveal blindingly white teeth flashing against her dark skin. Hattie swallowed, wondering how long she'd been behind her and how much she'd heard.

"Hattie, dear, I'll take Tucker back. You can go on back to stocking."

"Oh, okay," Hattie said softly, feeling disoriented.

"Great meeting you, Hattie," Tucker said, the picture of professionalism as he reached his hand out to shake hers one final time and then turned back to Matilda, who gave him a smothering embrace that he accepted with a measure of resignation.

"Good to see you, honey." Matilda latched on to his upper arm, her acrylic nails squeezing tightly as they grabbed a healthy fistful of his muscular tricep. "Let's get you all squared away." Pausing, she looked back over her shoulder at Hattie. "And, Hattie?"

Jerking her head up, Hattie widened her eyes. "Yes?"

"He really is kind of your boss, too."

"Oh, okay." She could feel her face burning with embarrassment. She glanced up briefly to see Tuck's smile widening to Cheshire proportions. "I understand." She trailed off lamely.

"Good!" Matilda said brightly. She turned back to Tuck. "Now, off we go."

Hattie walked slowly back to the supply closet, actually looking forward to locking herself inside its gloomy quietude for a change. She could feel the heat coming off her burning cheeks in waves. What else had Matilda heard? Either way, she—

Abruptly, she realized that Tuck had placed something in her hand, a subtle, smooth gesture nested inside his last handshake. She opened her tightly clenched fist, revealing a small, folded piece of paper. She looked down at it, unblinking, before she picked it open, already slightly sweaty from being enclosed in her palm.

It was a note.

With his number.

It was the strangest thing. Who even wrote notes anymore? On actual paper, too. Was he too poor to even afford a phone? She quickly dismissed that thought; he did have a job, obviously. And probably made more money than she did. And the number meant he had a phone. Still, it was strange.

And yet, stranger still, she found herself slipping the note carefully into her pocket rather than dumping it directly into the nearest waste bin. Walking back into the supply closet, she picked up the carton of adhesive bandages and began to unload its contents. Yet her mind was elsewhere.

She had suddenly made the perfect contact for finding out where the babies in the artificial wombs— where *her* baby, Jane—ended up, and yet she couldn't stop thinking about that moment Tuck had thrown back his head and laughed. It was an uproarious, perfectly carefree brand of unrestrained laughter, and it had made her sick with longing. She saw him in a new way now—she couldn't help it—for there was only one other person she had ever known who laughed like that, so boisterously and unabashed, and now, it was as if she were seeing a little part of him resurrect back to life.

Yes, maybe she would go out with him. To find out more information about Progenitor, sure, but as silly as it sounded, also because of that laugh. He was brash, handsome, strong, full of hearty, opinionated laughter. He was, well—

Just like her grandfather.

Right there, right on the half-opened carton of adhesives bandages, a poor salve for what truly ailed her, she knelt down, bowed her head against the box, and let the tears burst forth.

First, her grandfather, and then baby Jane. What would she ruin next with her selfish choices?

And the worst part, the part she hated about herself—if she could go back and do it over, she wasn't sure she would do anything differently.

Chapter Fifteen

Differential Calculus

"You what?" The barely disguised jealousy in her voice became more apparent. "You got his number?"

"I didn't ask for it." Hattie's voice came out in a mumble. "He just gave it to me."

"Mm-hmm." Sally-Anne arched an eyebrow, appraising her as if trying to determine whether she was some type of floozy who routinely hit on deliverymen while on the clock or not. Her gaze softened, and she smiled. "Well, I guess you guys did already know each other anyway, right?"

"Um, yeah." Hattie shifted from foot to foot, uncomfortable with where this line of questioning was headed. "Something like that."

"How did you say you met?"

"I didn't."

The eyebrow raise was back, and she gave a worldly-wise nod. "I see."

"No, no, not like that."

"Whatever, Hattie." Sally-Anne sighed, exasperated. She leaned back in the chair at the kitchen table, looking around the small room, as if assessing why someone would even bother to rent a place like this, even here in Philly, which Hattie realized, was certainly saying something. Sally-Anne's face brightened, and the front legs of the chair pounded to the ground as she leaned forward, eyes intent on Hattie's slouched form. "So, when are you going to call him?"

Hattie shook her head emphatically, not sure what she was planning or if it was just Sally-Anne being Sally-Anne. "I'm not—"

"Well, actually, that's a good point; you don't want to do that." She tilted her head back and stroked her chin as if attempting to solve a differential calculus problem. Against her better judgment, Hattie stifled a small giggle, causing Sally-Anne to eye her up suspiciously with a frown. "What? All I'm saying is that you don't want to be the one to call him first even if he gave you his number. Then, the dynamic's all wrong, but don't worry." She sat back in her chair, a smug smile on her face. "I can get word to him that you're interested."

Hattie felt her heart speed up. "Oh, I don't think—"

Looking up from her phone with the nimble deftness of a digital native, she smirked, flipping her stringy blonde hair behind her shoulder with a sassy head bob. "Too late," she said innocently. "It's already done."

Groaning, Hattie reached for her friend's phone, but Sally-Anne dangled it just out of reach on the other side of the table. "What did you do?"

A chime sounded, and Sally-Anne looked down at her phone. A slow smile spread across her glowing face, and she looked up triumphantly. "All set. Tonight at seven thirty. He'll pick you up."

"What?" Hattie almost fell out of her chair in her scramble to sit up straight. "Tonight? And you told him where I lived?"

"Relax, it's just a date." Sally-Anne scowled and then looked back at her phone. "I mean, you said you already knew each other, right?"

"Not well enough to just invite him over and to go out on dates with him!"

"Well, I—" Sally-Anne looked surprisingly chagrined. The expression on her face was so pitiful that, for a moment, Hattie even felt sorry for her before she remembered to be good and truly mad. Sally-Anne bowed her head before looking up with a sly smile. "He is wicked cute though, isn't he? Maybe he'll take you somewhere where he has to go shirtless…" Her voice trailed off, a dreamy look flitting across her features. "Like a pool or a beach or—"

"Wow, are you serious? You know this is Philadelphia, right?" Hattie shook her head, struggling to not think of a shirtless Tuck while still remaining mad at Sally-Anne. "You really are impossible."

With a shrug, Sally-Anne grabbed her purse and stood up. "Well, at least someone else knows about this hot little date of yours, and he knows it, so come on. It's not like he's just going to show up and strangle you or something when I know he's coming over." She paused, looking down at her phone as it chimed repeatedly before giving Hattie a hesitant yet irrepressible grin. "And, now, half the office does, too, so don't worry. If he's a serial killer, he'll have a lot of witnesses he'll need to take care of, too." She raised an eyebrow suggestively while biting the corner of her lip. "And I'm first on the list."

"Oh my." Hattie placed a hand over her mouth, biting back a tiny, darting laugh tickled upward by the fluttery feeling in her stomach. "You are just ridiculous," she began before she just gave up and shook her head slowly. How could she stay mad at someone like Sally-Anne?

"All right, well, I've got to run." Her phone chimed again, and she flashed a slightly guilty look at Hattie before she dashed out the door with a shout that she'd check in on her later to see how the date went and to wear something cute, maybe that red top from the other day, and a half-dozen other hurriedly shouted instructions that Hattie promptly ignored.

Still sitting in the chair at her lonely table for two, now all by herself, Hattie exhaled slowly. Being around Sally-Anne was exhausting; it was like encountering a whirlwind—lots of excitement and activity when you were swept up in it, but then after it moved on, you were just left with a headache and a big mess.

With a groan, she remembered that the red top was currently sitting in a wrinkled pile of clothes in the corner of her bedroom. At least she didn't have to feel guilty about not putting her clothes away in her dresser if she no longer owned a dresser, right? Maybe she could salvage it by letting it hang in the bathroom while she took a hot shower. The steam would practically iron out the wrinkles and creases. She busied herself with thoughts of preparation for the date tonight—if she was going to actually go through with this, then you'd better believe she was going to look good doing it—but mostly because she knew, if she took a moment to reflect on her last date—the one with that liar, that fake, that *taker* who had sent her down the path of this whole pregnancy mess— then she might just sink down into that pile of clothes in her room and never get up.

But giving up wasn't an option. And, whether she liked it or not, she had been, and still was, a mother.

And she needed answers.

Answers that Tuck had.

Chapter Sixteen

The Date

He arrived wearing a black polo and a smirk. Hattie quickly opened the door and hustled outside, closing the door quickly behind her before he could get more than a glance inside her messy apartment.

Raising an eyebrow, he exclaimed, "Not big on housecleaning, huh? That's a strike."

Hattie frowned. "A what?"

Moving on as if he hadn't heard her, he looked up and down her street. "And here I was, worried about you knowing *I* lived in a bad neighborhood."

"Hey, I don't—it's not so bad." Hattie felt flustered, already on the defensive, and strangely protective of the quirky little street that had been home to her and her grandfather all these years—and, yes, it had definitely deteriorated as of late, but still.

This date was off to a horrible start already, just as she'd feared.

She looked him in the eye. "I happen to like this neighborhood. And, yes, it's much nicer than that street where you live, if you even have a house over there, or maybe you just mooch off someone else and crash on their couch or something."

He laughed, seeming to think her insult genuinely funny. She frowned, although something inside of her soared a little, too; her grandfather had been like that, impossible to insult because he never took anything seriously. It had all been a big joke to him. Even at the end, with his illness, it had been beyond frustrating to get him to take it soberly, and he never did, not until the very end, when he begged her to think of herself.

And she had. Curse her, she had.

She frowned at Tuck. "And what's with all the insults? You're picking me up for a date and we haven't even made it to the sidewalk and you've already insulted my cleaning ability"—she paused, admitting a tiny smile—"or lack thereof, and my neighborhood. I can only guess what else you've got planned."

"I was just about to mention how gorgeous you looked." His eyes traveled shamelessly up and down her body before meeting her eyes with a frank stare. "A ratio of two to one, insults to compliments, is pretty good for a beautiful woman." His smile broadened, and she noticed a dimple on just his left cheek, the only thing asymmetrical about his otherwise classically, breathtakingly handsome face. "Really, you should actually take that as a compliment in itself. The hotter you are, the more you need to be put in your place." At this, he waggled an eyebrow suggestively, as if daring her to react.

She felt her skin flush, and she wanted nothing more than to slap him right now, put him in *his place*, but then again, that was probably just what he wanted, maybe exactly what he was hoping for.

Deciding not to take the bait, she took a deep breath and appraised him coolly. "So, Mr. Romance, where are we headed?"

"Follow me," he said, his face brightening. He extended a hand.

Against her better judgment, she took it, noticing for the first time, up close and walking down the sidewalk hand in hand, just how *well formed* he was. Proportionally, he was not only handsome, but also broad-shouldered, long-limbed, and trim-waisted. Bands of corded muscle stood out in stark repose on his forearms, but he looked athletic, not big and bulky like those meatheads who lifted weights endlessly. Tuck wasn't just convex bulges and swells, but he rippled with concave hollows and shadows, making her lips feel dry at the thought of those measurements in a different context.

For a few moments, they continued to walk along in companionable silence, each seeming to enjoy the elementary sensation of something as simple as holding hands with someone for the first time, getting used to the various ripples and whorls, the shapes and contours of someone else's skin, pressing in such close and extended contact, with the hand—the most nerve- and pressure-centric point of the body.

And—something else she was growing to like about Tuck—he didn't feel the need to fill each moment of silence with frivolous small talk. He was utterly confident in his own skin, and she liked that. He wasn't boring in the least, and though he could be quite grating, he never seemed to feel the need to entertain or earn her attention. He was just Tuck, take it or leave it. And, as a smart and attractive woman, one who was endlessly besieged with flirters and clingers, wannabe admirers who plagued her with trivial and pointless chatter, this silence was a refreshing twist.

Within minutes, Hattie's taste buds began to water as she smelled the stereotypical Philadelphian scent of cheesesteaks wafting on the wind. With a hopeful glance at Tuck, he nodded his assurance that cheesesteaks were, indeed, their intended destination, and they both picked up the pace. Internally, Hattie breathed a sigh of relief that this wasn't going to be some kind of formal, serious thing.

While their country and its government were going to pot and financial calamity—among many other variations—seemed ready to strike at any moment, Hattie thought wryly that it was a uniquely American form of dystopia that its citizens could walk down the street in total freedom to eat cheesesteaks and communicate on their phones, all the while complaining loudly of how hard they had it. And it was true, Hattie admitted; times were hard. There were real problems all around her, problems without easy answers; she couldn't remember the last time she could actually afford to go out to eat. But maybe it had always been that way. Americans were famous for not realizing that, in comparison to the rest of the world, even those who were considered "poor" by American standards, were, in fact, quite rich.

"Here we are." Tuck released her hand and walked straight up to the street side counter to order, seemingly as excited as she was to get a cheesesteak.

Hattie wondered if maybe this meal was the first time in a long time he would be eating out at a restaurant, too. Her heart softened a little at his earlier brashness; like her, he probably wasn't making a ton of money, working for MM, so the cost of this meal would mean something to him.

When it was their turn to order, Tuck stepped up confidently and hollered out, "Two Whiz Wit," showing that, while it might not be a regular occurrence, he was still a Philly native, knowing the lingo for two cheesesteaks with the gooey liquid-gold Cheez Whiz topped with onions. Thankfully, they were at a Pat's-style restaurant since she much preferred the "Whiz" over the provolone that some others, like Geno's, would offer—heretically, according to her grandfather.

After grabbing fries, Tuck made his way back to her, the triumphant smile of a victorious hunter bringing an armful of hard-won bounty gleaming on his face. "Here you are," he said, edging one aluminum-wrapped sandwich into her eager hands.

"This looks amazing," she exclaimed. And she meant it. No matter how the rest of the date went, in comparison to the white rice and canned pinto beans in her cupboards at home, this night was already a raging success. She looked up at him. "How'd you know how I wanted my cheesesteak?"

He shook his head. "This is the only way to get it. No Whiz, no onions—it's hardly even a real Philly cheesesteak then, is it?"

She nodded her agreement because she did concur with the sentiment, although what kind of guy just ordered what he expected her to eat without even asking her opinion? She arched an eyebrow. "What if I preferred provolone?"

His face instantly morphed into a mock-terrified look. "Heresy," he said matter-of-factly, causing Hattie to duck her face into her sandwich and take a huge bite to cover her shock at the memory of her grandfather. "What?" he asked curiously, noticing the look on her face. "It's not an unusual opinion. Every *real* Philadelphian knows that."

"Yeah," she said, trying to talk with her mouth full and feeling as if she were being transported directly into greasy cheesesteak heaven. "I know; I know. I've heard it a lot, too."

Hattie paused, mid-bite, noticing that he hadn't even taken his first bite but was just watching her eat with a look that was equal parts shock and outright joy with maybe even a hint of revulsion mixed in. Her face reddened as she lifted a nail to wipe orange goo off the corner of her lip, and then, unable to waste even a drop of the liquid gold, she sucked her fingertip clean. He seemed to enjoy watching her stuff her face, and to her shame, she knew it wasn't the first time she'd had a date watch her like an animal at the zoo while she ate.

"I-I'd say you like the way I ordered yours just fine," he finally said, his eyes shrinking down to normal size. Regaining his composure, he laughed. Eyes twinkling, he wiggled his eyebrows suggestively, grinning his shark grin that seemed to invite a slap— or something else. "I love a woman who loves to eat and doesn't look like she loves to eat."

"Was that a compliment?" Hattie frowned, still chewing. "Or an insult? I can't really tell which column that goes into, maybe one into each."

He popped a fry in his mouth. "So, anyway"—he tossed another fry up high into the air, and then, unperturbed at her frown, he caught it in his mouth and bowed grandly, as if to great applause—"even though you're halfway done with your sandwich already, I was thinking we could head down by the river, maybe watch and see if a boat might come by. It's just a few blocks down this way—"

"Oh, I know," Hattie interrupted, suddenly feeling embarrassed for devouring her sub so quickly. She set off at an industrious clip, crinkling aluminum foil with each step as she wrapped it up to keep it hot. "Let's go!"

Laughing, he jogged to keep pace with her. "You can keep eating your sub on the way, you know." He shook his head, looking at her sideways, green eyes glittering against the backdrop of old and worn-down Philadelphia-style row houses. "It's okay. Just eat it," he said gently, as if trying to hand-feed a tiger with fresh meat to keep it placated.

Feeling a little foolish but not willing to let her perfect cheesesteak grow cold, Hattie took another bite. "Thank you." She paused mid-bite, and she met his eye. "And, really, I mean it; thank you. This is delicious. I haven't had one of these in forever, not since—" Her eyes focused on something just over Tuck's left shoulder as an image of her grandfather—healthy and cackling boisterously as he walked along the sidewalk, waving his cheesesteak in the air while gesticulating wildly in the throes of one of his stories—almost made her eyes misty. Blinking quickly, she locked back in on Tuck. "Just not in a long time," she said quietly, looking down and then taking another, much smaller bite.

"Well, I'm glad we're doing this then," he said, unwrapping his sub for the first time. "And I'll eat mine, too, while we're walking." It was a kind gesture, and she smiled appreciatively at him. He spoke, and this time, his mouth was full, "And you passed the first and most important test; you like yours with Whiz and onion, not provolone or even worse, like those weirdos who go cheese-less." He frowned, a look of horror creeping across his handsome features. "I mean, who would want to even live like that, no cheese?"

She giggled, sucking a glob of congealing orange cheese-like substance off her fingertip with a smacking pop, as if to emphasize her agreement.

Within moments, they found themselves on the bank of the Delaware River, a sudden intrusion of nature among the dirty and overbuilt urban jungle that was the City of Brotherly Love. Hattie marveled at the swirling power of the dark, throbbing river, one of nineteen "Great Waters" recognized by the US—a fact her grandfather had endlessly been enthusiastic about as he would regal her with stories of history and commerce, business, and betrayal, the Delaware being an integral part of the nation's economic development, the site of everything from George Washington's famous crossing to William Penn's treaty with the Indians. Hattie's face grew distant as she gazed into the ever-flowing water, thinking of both her grandfather and the mighty river's fall from grace, now toiling to carry litter more so than important ships loaded with cargo, and a microcosm of the nation as a whole.

Tuck spoke softly, the ghost of a smile on his face, "Nothing like watching trash float slowly by to make for a romantic setting for a date, huh?"

Breaking her reverie, she turned from the water. "It's fine. It's perfect actually." Her gaze grew distant. "I have a lot of memories of being down here as a little girl."

He beamed. "I was hoping you'd like it." He paused, his face softening into a shy grin that seemed out of character for his usual cockiness. "You have your friend to thank for this more than me though."

"Sally-Anne?"

He nodded. "Yeah, figured I would tell you it was her idea now before she took all the credit later on anyway." A wry smile flickered across his face. "I don't think she's much for keeping secrets, that is."

"Ha. No, she's not," Hattie agreed. "She told you to bring me down here?"

"Well, I asked her what you liked to do, and she didn't really know, but"—his eyes grew soft, warm, and he held her gaze—"she said she remembered you talking about spending time down here with your grandfather, so..." He shrugged, his face blooming the slightest shade darker. "I just thought it might be nice, thought you might like it." His voice faltered, and he looked at her, seeming concerned that he had passed across some unspoken boundary.

"I do," Hattie said softly, brushing her fingertips across his shoulder. "I really do. I mean it. Thank you."

"Okay, well, good," he spoke quickly, seeming in a hurry to change the subject. "So, your grandfather—" He paused, seeming to realize that this was likely even more of a sensitive subject than his romantic planning. "I-I'm sorry. We don't need to talk about—"

"No, it's okay." Hattie rested her hand lightly on his forearm. "He passed away not too long ago." She spoke by rote, as if reading from a script, which, in some ways, maybe she was. She gulped, trying not to think about how much longer he might have lived had she not ... done what she had. "It was just us. He raised me. He was all I really had." Her mind raced. *It's not like I couldn't help him out of all that pain, right? What kind of life would that have been?* It wasn't what he'd wanted, not at the very end. "He was a great man," she said finally. "You would have liked him." Then, feeling silly at that last comment—after all, she hardly even knew Tuck; this was their first date, for goodness' sake, and here she was, already baring her soul to him—she blushed and looked at the ground.

Tuck's voice was low. "He certainly sounds like it. I think I would have liked him." His voice tinged with a pitch of humor. "*Especially* if he liked his cheesesteaks the real Philly way—*Whiz Wit.*"

She looked up with a quick smile, appreciating the levity. "Well, you guys would have loved each other then."

Her grandfather had been as alpha and as manly as they came, but he didn't take himself too seriously, and he wasn't like those overbearing, overprotective dads and father figures who came to the front door of their daughter's first date, wearing camo and cleaning their guns; no, his style was more like Tuck's: sly and clever, always cracking jokes and laughing, with an in-your-face, aggressive humor, testing you to see if you could give it as well as you could take it.

He would have liked Tuck's attitude, she thought.

He was annoying sometimes, sure, but like her grandfather, he had a way of saying the most ridiculously, outrageously insulting things with such panache, such a self-aware, *can you believe I'm gonna get away with this* good-natured flair that you couldn't help but just shake your head and laugh. A smile played across her features as she stared out at the river's dark depths again, collecting her thoughts.

She snuck a sideways glance at Tuck, who was taking the opportunity to give her a quiet moment's reflection on the water while he plowed into his cheesesteak with obvious relish, not even bothering to use a napkin. He even ate his cheesesteak in that gross, ultra-carefree, *my shirt might get ruined, and I don't even care way* that had been typical of her grandfather, too.

As she watched him eat, a sliver of guilt sliced across her conscience, causing her to wince and physically turn away. All this thinking of her grandfather made her think of what she'd done to him, and thinking of what she'd done to him made her think of what she'd done to baby Jane, and on it went, the never-ending circle of spiraling guilt.

But what choice did I have? she wanted to rage. Where was God when everything in her life was falling apart and there were no easy answers? Not for the first time, she wished she had someone she could talk to. She had done the best she could, but if that were true, why did she seem to live with this constant sense of permeating guilt?

She turned to see Tuck—cheesesteak finished and now watching her closely.

"What are you thinking about?" he asked quietly, taking her aluminum foil to add to his own, pounding and shaping it into a greasy little ball.

"Just regrets and mistakes," she sighed. "Shoulda, coulda, wouldas, lost hopes and missed opportunities, failures and busted dreams."

He cocked his head. "It's the Philly way." His voice was light, but he watched her carefully, maybe even tenderly, his green eyes glittering like a cat's against the dusking sky. "Us Philadelphians are good at all of the above." He winced. "And I don't mean just the sports teams." His gaze grew distant. "You're not the only one who misses someone," he said softly. "You have memories of your grandfather down here by the river, and I have mine of my dad." He swallowed, looking out over the river. "Our thing—if we even had a thing—was Sixers games." He smiled. "They were horrible, but it didn't matter because I got to spend time with my dad. And then—" His face twisted in a spasm of painful recollection. "And then he was just gone."

Her arm moved, as if by its own accord, and Hattie's hand gently caressed his neck, feeling powerful trapezius muscles tight with tension. "I'm sorry. I really am."

He looked over, and they locked eyes.

His mouth twitched into a sad, wistful smile. "At least we had that time together, and I can hold on to those memories. Some people don't even have that."

Hattie felt a swelling in her chest. "We can always find something to be thankful for," she parroted her grandfather's advice, watching Tuck carefully.

"That's right," he said, appearing taken back for a moment before his face relaxed back into that easy, confident smile of his. "We're both healthy, and we both have jobs; that's a lot more than most people in this city. We have places to sleep at night—even if you never clean your place, and I just sleep on someone's couch, that is."

The corner of her mouth lifted in a crooked smile. It was nice having someone around who could be sensitive and caring but also knew when a lighthearted comment would keep her from falling too hard into the pits. She'd missed that over the last two years. "I-I have a question for you," she said suddenly, locking in on his eyes.

"Okay," he said without blinking. "Ask away."

She took a deep breath. "Your job, your responsibility, is to take away the babies from MM and then, what, exactly?" She exhaled quickly, her mouth feeling dry all of a sudden.

"Well," he said, blinking, and looking uncertain as to where this line of questioning was heading, "sometimes, I get a requisition order for a pickup at MM during the day, like when you saw me the other day, but usually, the deliveries happen during the night—that's when most of the transportation is done—so they're back at the lab first thing the next morning for their—" His voice slowed, and he suddenly looked uncomfortable, stretching his collar while seeming to gather the courage to continue talking. "So, they're back to the lab for their, um, final procedure, and then harvesting."

Hattie swallowed, trying to control her furiously racing pulse, and nodded for him to continue.

He spoke more quickly, glad to be on firmer ground, "It's just that, sometimes, I have to shoot over quick and do a midday pickup, but usually, we try to avoid that—what with traffic being what it is and the protestors and all of that..." His voice trailed off, and he frowned slightly. "Why do you ask?"

Maybe it was her imagination, but his voice seemed colder, more detached, regaining a hint of the more professional- and business-sounding mannerisms she had noticed in him that first day in the lobby at MM.

She felt a rising panic swelling inside her. So, baby Jane was not necessarily even still at MM—at least, not in her building. She could be long-gone by now, taken away by cold and detached deliverymen grunting and sweating in the night, maybe even carting her away right this very moment.

Her pulse quickened. "I—" she started, not sure what exactly to say, but then—maybe it was all the memories and flashbacks of her grandfather, maybe it was her natural tendency to sabotage anything good that ever happened to her, or maybe it was just the way the quickly darkening sky—twilight, in their ruined and soiled ecosystem seemingly cursed and stained forever, seemed to portend a looming menace. She didn't know. She decided to do the easiest thing—just tell the truth. She cleared her throat. "I'm looking for a particular baby. Well, looking to see what will happen to it anyway." Her voice sounded foreign to her ears; it squeaked out tiny and hoarse.

"Oh," he said, his hand pausing mid-throw from tossing the little aluminum foil ball up and down. His brow wrinkled up, and he just looked at her, assessing her, maybe judging her. He began to lightly toss the ball again, regaining his usual composure. "There are ways to find out. But it's not easy, and it's obviously, um—" He coughed delicately. "It's not entirely legal. I could maybe look into it for you. I could try anyway, but..." He paused, his eyes never leaving hers. "Are you sure it's worth it? I mean, this fetus, um, this baby..." He swallowed, and then said tentatively, "This baby is special to you?"

"Yes."

He cocked his head, a puzzled look on his face.

She took a deep breath, closing her eyes. She had to tell him. And the date, to her great surprise, had actually been going so well, too. Well, he was sure to find out eventually anyway.

She opened her eyes and held his gaze. "It's mine."

Chapter Seventeen

Even If It Hurts

It's disorienting, going from here to there and back again, all so quickly and without warning. Not to mention, the emotions swirling around from all that I'm experiencing *over there* and now still trying to process.

He seems to sense this, his face sympathetic and kind, those great golden eyes shining like lustrous, freshly polished golden balls, depthless and fathomless. For the first time—with his gaze so intent on me as I awake that it's almost predatory—I'm struck by how ferocious and scary he might look in a different context. But his smile broadens as he makes eye contact with me, and I breathe a little sigh of relief. Though he has never spoken in anything but soft, gentle tones, I get the sense that he is not someone to be trifled with. He's used to giving instructions, not suggestions; that much is certain.

"You're back," he says simply, his eyes seeming to pick up all the shimmery golds and purples around us and refract them back to me via his intense gaze.

I shrug, not knowing what to say. "Yep."

He doesn't blink, and his large, handsome face is statuesque. He stays in repose, not moving a muscle. I get the strangest sense he knows what's going to happen to me next, *over there*, and he's not happy about it.

I swallow, glad he's on my side.

I think.

"So," I start off, hoping he'll fill the silence.

He does. "If you want to see this through, to the end, then you need to go back." It comes out all in a flood. "But, if you don't want to, if you can't finish," he adds quickly, his eyes never leaving my face, "you don't have to. Just say the word."

For the first time since being back this time, I am cognizant of the belt across my lap. It feels restraining, and part of me bucks against the sensation. It's not how things are intended to be *here*; that's for certain. It's very clearly a remnant of *over there*. And yet I know I need to finish what I started.

I have to know.

How it ends.

He smiles a sad smile, full of depths I'll puzzle over later. What all does he know? One thing he does know though is that I want to go back. I need to go back. He doesn't even need to hear me say it out loud.

"There's pain there," he says. "Not like here."

"I know," I say quietly. Oh, I know.

"Suffering, too. And no one to wipe the tears away." His voice is flat.

He's already resigned himself to having his advice go unheeded. Maybe this is new for him. Something inside me feels guilty for some reason.

"Yeah," I say. "I can still kind of feel it." I cock my head, genuinely confused. "Well, maybe not. I can't feel it right now. But I know it's there." I pause and then clarify, "Well, *over there* anyway. And there's a lot of it." I meet his eyes, wanting him to understand.

He nods that he does.

As the red button is pressed and I'm slipping away once again, I think, *Why didn't I just ask him what was going to happen next? Why not ask him if he thinks I should go back or not?*

Because I know what his answer would be, I tell myself.

And it doesn't matter anyway. I'm doing this for me, not for him.

I close my eyes and let myself be pulled back under.

My last thought, like a wisp of smoke curling up in faint tendrils and dissipating skyward, is this: *I just have to know; that's why.*

Even if it hurts.

Chapter Eighteen

Code 468

Hattie walked down the sidewalk on her way to work, still thinking about the last few days.

Tuck had done as he'd said; he'd done his best to get some info on her baby. Had it just been her imagination, or had Tuck treated her differently? His answers about Hattie's baby had been short and curt; he had spoken to her almost robotically with about as much passion as one of the TED units. Maybe it was all in her mind though. Was she just projecting her own desire for dispassionate, pragmatic decision-making onto him?

His eyes though—those green, fathomless eyes. He had been quiet, but his eyes seemed to speak volumes. They had been soft, kind, reaching out to her, not judging her. Or had she just imagined that, too?

Maybe he had been short and curt because she had been short and curt. Maybe he'd sensed that she just didn't want to go into the details and given her space. It was, after all, not really any of his business. She sighed. That was, until she had *made* it his business.

One thing she just couldn't do though: she couldn't bring herself to tell him or anyone else that she had named her Jane. It just sounded so foolish; you didn't name a baby you'd aborted.

She shook her head wryly, bowed and bent against the wind as her hair blew like streamers behind her. What kind of girl went out on a date with a guy and then decided that things were going so well that she should spring something like, *Hey, just so you know, I just got pregnant not too long ago by some guy I don't want to talk about, and I just had an abortion. Oh, and can you risk your job and your career to help me feel better about my poor decisions?* But, to his credit, he had done that, although to no avail.

She didn't have any more information about baby Jane than she had before.

But…

He had told her how she could find out.

Matilda.

All of those requisition orders—yes, on actual paper; *gotta love the medical field and their antiquated love for paper*, Hattie had thought—were locked away somewhere in Matilda's office, just waiting for their transit dates—that much he knew. Plus, as she had learned in training, ever since the Great Internet Blackout years back—a worldwide internet outage for eleven days, resulting in countless fatalities, an unprecedented panic, and in many ways was a greater disaster than World War V—a flurry of hastily drawn regulations, like the Medical Record Universal Document Retrieval Act (abbreviated as MURDR—the unfortunate acronym proof of just how quickly politicians had moved to pass something) mandated paper backups of key records in many important industries, including hospitals and ancillary medical facilities, of which Managed Motherhood was included. So, though electronic records were firewalled and monitored aggressively for hackers, she knew their paper duplicates simply sat in folders in Matilda's office.

The sinking feeling in the pit of her stomach grew, and her step faltered as she skipped around a chasm in the sidewalk. Now, it was her turn to risk her job.

She had planned it all out. Today, when the coast was clear and Charles was in full-on flirting mode, she would break into Matilda's office and finally get some answers.

Because she just had to know.

Walking in the front door of MM, she hardly even noticed the protestors. Once inside, she took a deep breath. Lifting a tentative hand at Sally-Anne, she nodded politely at her.

Sally-Anne's eyes sparkled with a roguish glint as she stayed uncharacteristically quiet, shuffling paperwork around on her desk to appear busy. She inclined her head slightly to point out to Hattie that Matilda was close by and within earshot. The smooth baritone sounds of Charles's ever-present flirtations wafted just around the corner and Sally-Anne rolled her eyes.

With a little smile, Hattie stepped through the interior door and into the hallway to find herself suddenly alone and with a clear shot to Matilda's office.

The vein in her neck seemed to pound with a pulsing, furious intensity, and she felt blood rushing in her ears. Was now a good time? Should she just go with it? Charles's and Matilda's early morning pastry routine could last for a while, and this might be the best chance she would get all day.

In a flash, she made the decision and set off down the hallway, bouncing lightly on the balls of her feet. Time to get this over with.

Slowing at Matilda's office door, she glanced up and down the hallway, tugged on the handle to find it unlocked, jerked on it, and darted inside. Her breath came in swollen gasps, and she had the absurd thought that she would make a horrible cat burglar. She forced herself to slow her breathing; it would hardly do to keel over from a heart attack right here at the scene of the crime.

She walked around behind the desk and started at the top left corner, opening drawers and quickly leafing through the sheaf of papers. She had an excuse ready—*Oh, Matilda, there you are. I was just looking for a piece of paper to leave you a note. I need to request some time off for next Friday*—but it was flimsy at best, and she knew it. Jamming the papers back in the drawer in some semblance of the way she'd found them, she moved on to the right side of the desk, her heart still beating like a runaway snare drum.

And then she hit pay dirt—a canary-yellow folder marked Requisition Orders, stuffed with loose papers, a laminated card with a table listing out medical procedure codes affixed to the front of the folder. Hurriedly, she paged through the papers, sitting down in Matilda's chair in her haste. Thankfully, they were arranged numerically by patient code, so it was quick work to find her patient number.

Holding the folder open on her lap, the requisition order with her patient number in the top-right corner seemed to shout up at her, *Look what you've done, look what you've done*—formal documentation of all her mistakes. First: her initial mistake with *him.* Second: her mistake to harm the only innocent party in the entire situation—her baby. And, now, all she wanted to do was fix her mistake.

She looked at the scheduled transfer time and date.

12:00 midnight.

Tonight.

She breathed a short sigh of relief, happy that baby Jane was still in the building, but then just as quickly, she felt her heart beat quicken. Not for long. She was being transported tonight—in less than sixteen hours.

Not that it even matters, she thought. She had already made the choice to get rid of her, forced her out when her baby needed her, and now, it was too late. But still, she wanted to know what was going to happen to her. That much she could do for her.

She drew her fingertip slowly along the form, tracing each line until stopping at the Medical Code box: *468*. Slowly, she closed the folder, moving her finger down the laminated printout on the front, starting in the first column—*465, 466, 467*—and then her finger came to a rest at *468*. Sliding over to the adjacent column, she read the description.

Intact late-term organs requested, extremities to medical waste, D&C authorized.

Shoulders slumping, she put the folder back in the drawer and walked out of the office in a trance, long past even caring who saw her. She might be new to MM, but she knew what a D&C abortion was—sharp, cutting instruments scraping and scooping to clean out small body parts from inside the uterus. And all just so that the torso and its valuable internal organs could be harvested and sold, the arms and legs tossed in the trash. It was not atypical that appendages were dismembered from the small body within the body and, in fact, was often a necessity, given the size and shape of the torso and skull. Sometimes, the size of the skull was such that it had to be cratered in, the tiny brains vacuumed out like so much medical waste.

Hurriedly, she ran to the restroom and locked herself in a stall, bending over at the waist to fight back great, racking sobs.

She tried to tell herself that everything would be all right.

This too will pass. This too will pass. She repeated the mantra over and over, feeling strangely comforted by those glossy, superficial brochures from the waiting room.

And yet, deep down, in that protected little part of her that she never allowed anyone to see, she knew it was a lie. A sham. She was not all right. What she'd done was not right. She had turned her back on baby Jane when she needed her, when she trusted her, when she was as close to her as she could possibly be to another human being.

Her back rose and fell, and she struggled to regain her composure. One thing bothered her though. *Why would they even need to do a D&C procedure?* The baby, along with the womb, was already out of her body; it wasn't like they needed to probe around and scrape anything out of her. The baby was already out—

And then it came to her—a snippet of a long-ago memory from when the debate had been front and center in the news when she was just a child. Was it something a talking head on a news program had said? Or—she swallowed—maybe a comment her grandfather had made? It was a facade, a technicality, a way to stay within the legal parameters of the agreed-upon abortion, but just to prolong the timing of the procedure in a way that was most beneficial to MM.

And to her, the patient, if she were being honest, that much was certainly helpful. D&C procedures, and even the safer vacuum aspiration procedures, were not without their risks to the mother—it was far from a natural thing to violently sever this, the most sacred and essential of bonds, that of mother and baby—and so, just removing the baby and womb intact, all at once, had to have far fewer side effects than the scraping and vacuuming for body parts as with the old procedures. It was better for everyone.

Well, almost everyone.

Everyone, except for baby Jane.

She fought back another tremor.

Hearing the sound of the restroom door whoosh open, Hattie whirled around, attempting to prevent herself from being seen through the crack in the stall partition. Holding her breath, she could hear tentative footsteps pattering in and then stopping just outside the stall.

"Hattie?" Sally-Anne's breathless voice whispered. "Is that you?"

Hattie fought back a sniffle and a groan at the same time.

"Hattie, I know that's you." A pause and then a sigh. "Hattie, I can see your feet."

Scooching her feet back slightly, Hattie hoped in vain that Sally-Anne would get the hint and just go away. She hugged her arms across her chest and looked down at the floor, as if giving in to the childish impulse that, if you closed your eyes, no one would see you.

"Come on, Hattie." Another sigh. "Plus, I can see you through the crack."

Hattie jerked her head up, wiping a tear-stained cheek furiously, to see one of Sally-Anne's heavily mascaraed eyes staring at her, unblinking, through the space where the door met the stall wall.

"What-what is your problem?" she mumbled, still wiping her eyes. "Can't anyone get some privacy around here?"

"Sorry." Sally-Anne shrugged. "But I needed to find you."

Hattie frowned. "What is so important that it can't wait until—"

"Hattie, listen," Sally-Anne interrupted. "Matilda's looking for you. She said something about—well, I don't know, but it didn't sound good." Her voice was soft. "I think you're in trouble. Big trouble."

Hattie opened the door slowly, the color draining from her face. Her mind raced. Had she put everything back where she had found it in the office? Had someone seen her? "What do you mean?"

Sally-Anne glanced down at her feet. "And, um, I'm sorry, but I think she knows about you going back into the womb room to see, um, your, you know."

"What do you mean, *you think she knows*?" Hattie took a step closer. "What did you tell her?"

"Listen, Hattie, I'm sorry." Sally-Anne's voice stretched and strained. "I'm really sorry, I am, but this job is important to me. I really need this job. I didn't mean to hurt you or get you in trouble, but—"

"Well, you did!" Hattie stamped her foot, eyes flashing, forgetting her sadness or worry about what Matilda was going to say. "You did get me in trouble, and you did hurt me. Just—" Hattie shook her head, all the frustrations and disappointments in herself coming out in a flood on Sally-Anne. "Just leave me alone. I don't want to talk to you, and I don't want to see you."

Sally-Anne's face fell, looking like a pitiful puppy seeing a rolled-up newspaper appear in its master's hand. "Okay," she said softly, turning back to the door. She stopped, started to speak, and then seemed to reconsider. Finally, as she reached the door, she looked over her shoulder, speaking quickly, and not making eye contact, "Matilda wants to see you in her office."

The door swished shut with a hydraulic whoosh, seeming to take with it all of the air from Hattie's lungs.

Hattie stood, alone in the harsh fluorescent lighting of the clinic restroom, fighting the urge to curl up in a ball in the corner and cry. Well, if she was going to get fired, she was going to do it with her head held high and her pride intact. She looked into the mirror, using a wet paper towel to blot away makeup smudges from her tear-stained eyes. Slowly, she stood up straight and steeled herself for the task ahead.

Of course she needed this job—hadn't Sally-Anne thought about that, how much she needed this job, too?—but she'd been through much worse than getting let go from a job; that was for certain. An image of her grandfather, the pride he would've felt at this, her first real job, one that could translate into an actual career, and then his subsequent disappointment at her recent actions: getting pregnant, having an abortion, going on a date with some other guy soon after, and now this, most likely being fired from MM.

What kind of person had she become? She looked in the mirror one last time, set a mask of placid and studied neutrality to disguise her true feelings, and walked out the door.

In mere moments, she stood outside Matilda's office door, her heart beating even faster than it had just moments earlier when she found herself in this same location. Slowly, she lifted a tentative hand and knocked lightly.

"Come in." Matilda's voice boomed out instantaneously. "Hi, Hattie," she said as the door opened. "Come in and sit down, please."

Hattie licked her lips and then eased herself into a chair in front of Matilda's desk. "You wanted to see me?"

Ignoring the question, Matilda met her eyes with an unyielding gaze. "Thank you for knocking." She paused. "*This time.*"

Hattie swallowed. In sharp contrast to the bead of nervous sweat that trickled down her spine, her mouth felt dryer than dry, and she struggled to form a coherent sentence. "I-I just—I was just—"

Matilda held up a large, long-nailed hand. "Don't," she said authoritatively. "I know you were in my office without my permission." She held up the yellow Requisition Orders folder. "And I know you were looking through this."

Sitting stock-still, Hattie saw something in Matilda's eyes that warned her against trying to talk her way out of what she'd done; she needed to come clean. "I'm sorry," she said, hanging her head. Her voice was small. "You're right."

Matilda's gaze softened, and Hattie was reminded again of the kind, maternal way that Matilda had treated her ever since she first started working for MM, which only made her feel that much worse about what she'd done, of course.

"Well," Matilda began slowly, "what you did was wrong, but I can't say I don't sympathize with your position." She set the yellow folder gently on the desk. "And I understand why you did what you did; I know that you didn't do it for malicious reasons."

Hattie lifted her head, daring to meet Matilda's eyes. "Oh, thank—"

"Wait," Matilda said, hoping up a large hand again. "I'm not finished."

Swallowing, Hattie nodded, trying not to shift around in too guilty of a manner in the uncomfortable, straight-backed office chair.

"So, just because I understand your motivation and maybe even sympathize with it—you just found out you were pregnant, then you had an abortion, all within the past month or so. It's not easy, I know, and you're still trying to adjust, I get that." Matilda tapped her index finger insistently on the desk and then suddenly stopped, exhaling a long breath in a sudden rush of world-weariness that made her look ten years older. "And, partially, this is my fault. I still—" She sighed and gave her head a tiny shake. "I still feel horrible about what happened with the TED scan; I really do. That wasn't fair to you at all. But still"—she looked meaningfully at Hattie—"that does not give you the right to just flout the rules we have around here."

"I understand."

"So here's what we're going to do." She steepled her long-nailed fingers and leaned back in her chair. "We're going to take some time, right now, and work through this. You didn't get the clear explanations you needed before your TED scan, and I take full responsibility for that, but now, we are going to talk this through. I want you to ask me anything you want, so we can move past this and get back to working together with trust and understanding." Her dark eyes shone warmly at Hattie, her face a picture of maternal concern. "What do you think? Can we do that?"

"Okay," Hattie said.

"Good." Matilda lifted her hands wide. "Well, ask away. I've found it's always best to get your questions out in the open." With a snort, she inclined her head. "God knows those protestors out front aren't afraid to voice their concerns." She looked back at Hattie. "But, really, it's always better to talk about it, talk about how you're feeling, and that's something we can always do better with our patients; I realize that."

"Well …" Hattie began hesitantly, looking down at her lap and tracing the outline of her kneecap through her scrubs. She looked up suddenly. "I think I made a mistake."

Matilda nodded. "You're not the first. Why do you think you feel that way?"

"I-I just feel like—" Hattie swallowed. "I just feel like I let her down."

"You let—"

"My baby," Hattie finished. "I let my baby down. When she needed me most, I turned my back on her." Her voice turned into a small, twisted echo of itself, and not recognizing the sound sent a tiny tremor of fear quivering up her spine. "And, now, it's too late."

"Going back into that room, the womb room," Matilda began kindly but matter-of-factly, "you shouldn't have done that. There's a reason we don't publicize the external womb gestation technique. It interferes with the closure process." She sighed. "And that's what you're struggling with; it's very understandable."

"But I think I made a huge mistake!" Hattie's voice came out in a wail that shocked her; not until this very moment of speaking it out loud—at this, the importance of verbalizing, Matilda was right—had she realized just what she wanted. Her voice grew in pitch. "I just want my baby back!"

Calmly, Matilda nodded, the only movement on her face a tiny knitting of her eyebrows. "I understand," she said softly.

Hattie realized that Matilda had likely had this same conversation with literally hundreds of post-abortive women, hormonally desperate and volatile, not sure what to do, their emotions seesawing them wildly from one extreme to another. But she wasn't like them, was she? How could she make her see the difference?

At last, Matilda spoke again, "Tell me, Hattie, why did you decide to have the abortion in the first place?"

With a sniffle, she fought to rein her emotions under control. "Because it's the only decision that makes any sense. I have nothing," she sobbed. "Look at me! I'm a mess." On some level, she knew that baring her soul like this, to her boss, airing all her dirty laundry, was not a wise decision, but on another level, she couldn't care less. Go ahead and let them fire her; what did she care?

She slumped in her seat, feeling like a ball of tangled yarn slowly unraveling. "I can't take care of a baby," she said, her voice now quiet. "I can hardly even take care of myself." She looked up suddenly at Matilda, her eyes wide. "And that's why I appreciate this job so much—I really do—but I've had to just scrape by for so long." She swallowed, an unbidden thought of her grandfather serving her half of a brick of ramen noodles and ushering her to their flimsy card table with the flourish of a maître d' in the fanciest restaurant in town flashed across her memory with the force of a punch. "And, now, it's just me and the father's not in the picture and things were just starting to look up with this job, so—"

Matilda leaned forward and gently cut off her ramblings with an extended hand, "So, it sounds like you made the right decision." She leaned back, her eyes still warm and caring. "It's okay, Hattie. Regret is natural. Many won't admit it, but it happens all the time." She leaned forward again. "But the important thing is that you know you made the right choice."

For whom? Hattie wanted to ask, thinking of the choice denied to the tiny body floating in amniotic fluid in the womb room, but she bit her tongue.

There was a limit to how far she could test this boss-employee relationship, regardless of Matilda's sympathetic ear and her guilt at the TED scan, so she just nodded.

Watching her closely, Matilda spoke in soft undertones, "Things will get better; they really will. I've spoken to more women in your exact position than I can even count. It will get better." She rose from her chair. "But, right now, what you need is to take a little time and get your thoughts together."

Following her lead, Hattie rose to her feet, uncertain of what Matilda meant. She swallowed, "Um, okay."

"So, I want you to take the rest of the day off." Matilda placed a large forearm on her shoulder, ushering her to the door. "Go home, get some rest, and then come back tomorrow, ready to work." She paused, looking Hattie square in the eye. "How does that sound?"

"Fine," Hattie mumbled. "I mean, thank you."

The grip on her shoulder tightened. "And, Hattie?"

"Yes?"

"This time, we'll chalk up your, um, exploring to a misunderstanding, but there will be no next time. Are we clear?"

Hattie swallowed, understanding perfectly. "Of course."

Stumbling out of MM, purposefully avoiding Sally-Anne's hurt, puppy-dog face and barely seeing the protestors on the curb, she found herself arriving at her street without even realizing where the last minutes had gone. She just wanted to crawl in bed, maybe take a shower, and then—

She stopped abruptly, her gaze frozen on the figure leaning jauntily against the doorframe of her apartment. Hearing her feet scud to a stop on the sidewalk, the figure slowly turned to face her, that old, familiar, devil-may-care sneer splitting his handsome face into a cocky grin and causing her heart to rocket up into her throat.

Offset against skin so black, it was almost shades of blue, his large, extraordinarily white teeth flashed and sparkled in a ray of stray sunlight. "Hey, Hattie," he said easily, his voice carrying that note of familiarity and comfortable possession over her body that she had once craved.

"You…" Hattie narrowed her eyes, suddenly energized out of her tired stupor with the white-hot flame of righteous anger. "How dare you—"

Mildly, he glanced from side to side, as if to indicate the proximity of any possible nosy neighbors. "Relax," he said and then inclined his head to her door. "Can we talk inside?" He paused, a strange smile stretching across his features, one that Hattie had never seen before. This unnerved her, for she had thought that, at one time, she had every facial expression of his intimately cataloged and labeled. "It's about the baby," he said, his voice slowing into a measured drawl, coal-black eyes flashing. "*Our* baby."

How does he know about the baby?

Wordlessly, Hattie brushed by his shoulder and unlocked the door, her mind churning furiously until, finally, the only possible answer clicked into place, and she mentally excoriated Mrs. T for her loose lips.

But Mrs. T was Mrs. T.

She needed to deal with the larger problem right on her front porch.

He knew.

The taker, the stealer of her body and her heart, the one who had taken her apart and laid her soul bare for the world to see and then just left. The one who had taken what he wanted and then disappeared as casually as a one-night stand. But it hadn't been that, not to her. It had meant something. But, now, he was back, and he would be forced to confront the reality that their act had meant something beyond his fleeting pleasure; something special had happened: *someone* special.

Exhaling a long, tired sigh, she opened the door and motioned for Jane's father to come inside.

Chapter Nineteen

Here and There

The space between worlds thins. The *here* and *there* seem to become something else entirely, and I find myself floating between the two, confused and uncertain. Am I caught in the middle somehow? Maybe something has malfunctioned. My mind instantly goes to that red button, seemingly so long ago, but then I dismiss the thought. One look at his great golden eyes, and you know things didn't just "malfunction." That seems as implausible as saying the atmosphere around me is populated with square circles or round squares. Once you know anything about the perfect, wonderful *here*, then you know that just doesn't make any sense.

The sense of panic intensifies, and it is only now that I realize—the emotions welling up inside, the pain, the heartache, the worry, I can feel them all building like a tidal wave inside of me—those caring golden eyes aren't anywhere around. Therefore, I have to still be *there*.

This is such a different feeling than I remember over *there* to be though: cold, dark, entombing, the sense of swirling, eddying weightlessness. And yet it seems more real than before, as if I am seeing things from my unique vantage point for the first time. I flex my fingers and toes, attempting to gain some reassurance from the steadying proprioception of my body moving in space and do so but with small comfort. My heartbeat feels small in my chest, but oh-so fast.

Just as I feel the almost undeniable urge to cry out, I hear voices.

They grow closer.

Businesslike tones. Carefree. Matter-of-fact. Something about this scares me more than the uncertainty of whose voices those professional-sounding tones belong to.

They have a job to do.

And they are coming still closer.

The panic rises in my throat, and I fight through a sudden choking sensation brought on by the rush of anxiety. Kicking out, my foot makes contact with something slippery, and my mouth moves to make a silent scream—

And then, suddenly, light floods all around me. And peace, the sudden soothing of it washing over me in steady, calming waves, slowing my heartbeat down and causing my jaw to unclench.

I look down.

The belt stretches across my lap.

I'm-I'm back *here*? This has never happened before, not so abruptly, but I'm certainly not going to complain. The remnant of those racing feelings from over *there* still lingers somewhere just below my consciousness, and yet I know they are there.

"Are you okay?"

I look up so quickly, a strand of hair flops over my eyes like ill-shapen bangs. Those great golden eyes shine with piercing intensity. With a relieved smile, I feel my face suddenly relax—never have I been so glad to see him—and with a quick gust of breath, I blow the hair back where it belongs.

"I-I think so," I say softly. "What happened?"

His face grows even more serious. The way his eyebrows descend over his eyes gives the strange and sudden impression of storm clouds fast approaching over the horizon. He swallows, seeming to find it difficult to talk all of a sudden. This is new, and despite the lingering doubts and uncertainties of my emotions, I perk up with interest.

He speaks slowly, as if measuring out each word, "Well, I just thought you were having a difficult time of it, so"—a shadow of something that looks strangely like guilt appears briefly on his face and then disappears—"I just brought you back over *here*, just for a moment."

"Oh," I say, not sure if I should thank him or question him.

I do neither, and he responds before I can think of what to say, "It's getting really close to the end." His voice rumbles in a low warning that seems to say the storm is indeed approaching. "It's going to get, um…" He looks uncertain, not an expression that I ever imagined seeing across his normally self-composed features.

"Yes?" I say gently, prodding him on.

"It's going to get difficult," he says at last, eyeing me with concern, tenderness, and maybe even—dare I say it?—love.

I look closer at his eyes. Yes, definitely. I'm not mistaken. A protective, familial love. He doesn't come right out and say it, but it's there. He's not touching me, but it's as if his enormous arms are encircling me, wanting me to know that I'm treasured, that I'm important, that I'm not forgotten.

This scares me more than his warnings, for he must know I'll need this degree of fortification before finishing with whatever is about to happen over *there*.

Still, I swallow, steeling myself to finish what I started seemingly so long ago when I first pressed that red button.

"I'm ready," I say.

"Okay," he says so gently, it's as if he knows I am not ready, will never be ready, but he's turning me free anyway. As if he's caressing a tiny bird's broken wing, sheltering it from the gales and storms of the dark, blustery world but then forced to turn it loose into the swirling black skies to fend for itself. "You can go now."

And then, just as I'm giving myself over to the now-familiar, insistent tugging of sleep, the separator between these worlds, he says something so quietly I almost don't catch all of it, "I'm so sorry for what's going to happen next. I would stop it if I could. But I can't."

Chapter Twenty

Daddy Issues

"I just can't believe you would do something like that!" He slammed the cup down, water sloshing over the brim and causing the flimsy card table to sway erratically. His eyes narrowed. "And you didn't even tell me?"

"You left," Hattie said simply, turning from her kitchen sink and attempting to lift her cup of water to her lips without it shaking. "You took what you wanted, and then you just left." Hattie set the cup down carefully and looked him in the eye. "I was all alone."

He lifted his eyes and met her gaze. "I had to find out I was a father from Mrs. T."

"*You left*," Hattie drew the words out, like she was slowly raking his flesh across burning coals. "You left me." Her lip curled up. "You left *us*."

His thumb protruding like a club, he waggled it back at his chest assertively, enunciating every word. "But *I'm the father*, you should have consulted with me."

Hattie snorted, feeling her temper flare. "I should have *consulted with you*? And what does that mean, Mr. Take What You Want And Then Leave? You think you're some kind of Superdad now? You can't even stick around for me, let alone a child."

"I still should have known." His face turned morose, and despite herself, though she hated herself for it—she really did—Hattie felt sorry for him. His voice sounded far away. "I didn't even get a chance to stick around."

Her voice tiny, Hattie tried to keep the desperation out of the question. "Would you? Would you have stayed?"

Sighing, he placed the cup back down on the table, softly this time. "I don't know, Hattie. I just don't know." He stood and began pacing. "I guess we'll just never know."

For some strange reason, she found herself wanting to apologize to him, but she bit her tongue, a feeling of bright, white-hot fury rising inside her.

No.

She would not apologize for his irresponsibility.

No.

No.

NO.

He was the deadbeat who had walked out, not her. And she was not going to give in to his mind games to try to make her feel bad.

Still…looking at his strong, handsome face, she couldn't just *not* see all of their memories, all of their shared history together, could she? This unwanted sympathy welling up inside her—she hated it, hated herself for allowing it inside her, and it sparked another bright fuse of anger.

She shook her head. "Keon, please. *I* would have been the one who was pregnant for nine months, not you. *You left.* Not me. *You left.*"

The muscles in his jaw bunched, and he turned his dead-eyed stare onto her. "Well, I'm here now."

She sighed, suddenly feeling very tired, and said softly, "Well, you're too late."

Glowering, he eyed her as if she were an obstacle to be overcome, and it sent a thrill of fear up her spine. She was used to seeing him look at her as an object to be possessed—that was his way—and there had been a time when that sent a different kind of thrill through her body.

But, now, her mind kept returning to those instances while they had been dating, when his anger had been directed onto others who had unfortunately happened into his way—and with devastating results.

Looking back, of course, that should have been one of the first major warning signs. His emotional makeup was a high-proof cocktail of charm, lust, and aggression—intoxicating and exhilarating at the first, but the unavoidable hangover was a sullen disregard for anyone's feelings but his own.

And—watching him turn his hard-eyed stare out the window, as if daring someone to confront him— she was all too aware that he was a genuinely dangerous man. He and his cousins, who weren't really his cousins, were loosely affiliated with the Philadelphia Black Mafia crew who ran the corner of K&A, the notorious Kensington and Somerset to Alleghany intersection in the heartland of the Philadelphia Badlands, a cornucopia of the City of Brotherly Love's most base pleasures, drugs, and disordered affections, and a constant turf battle between the PBM, the Irish K&A Gang, the Latin Kings, and various motorcycle gangs.

His brows furrowed as he squinted against the glare of the last-remaining sunlight of the day streaming through the blinds. "Who's this cocky-looking, green-eyed pretty boy walking up your drive?"

A flutter of fear tickled up the inside of her chest, constricting her throat and bringing her hand reflexively to cover her gaping mouth. Green eyes? What was Tuck doing here again—and so soon? Her mind racing, she tried to think of any way this wouldn't quickly turn into an unmitigated disaster.

"I-I don't know," she spluttered, thinking that maybe, if she could somehow convince him not to answer the door, then Tuck would just give up and go away.

"This guy right here is walking up like he knows you or something." Keon's broad features widened in astonishment as a shadow seemed to fall across his face like the movement of a dark spirit, and he whirled to look at Hattie. "Does he?" he questioned, his voice with the deadly stillness of a coiled cobra. "Does he know you, Hattie?"

Seeming to find what he was looking for in her face, his lip curled up into a sneer. "Does he make himself at home here, Hattie, maybe right in your bed?"

Another tremor, like the sizzle of an electric current, raced from her torso to her extremities. A small whimper escaped her lips. She remembered this feeling. She remembered this look in his eyes.

A knock sounded on the door.

Keon held Hattie's gaze just long enough to smile that wicked, dominating smile of his, and with two big strides, he flung the door open.

Tuck stood at the door and frowned, appearing taken aback. "Who are you?"

"Who are *you*?" Keon growled, his shoulders bunching up aggressively.

They stood there, in the threshold of her tiny apartment, looking like two attack dogs encountering each other for the first time. If their ears could have laid flat, they would have. Not an eye blinked or a muscle moved, just that testosterone-driven alpha instinct to dominate and possess.

Not unlike the animal kingdom, Hattie thought, her sense of despair growing.

They were a study in contrasts. Where Keon was large, barrel-chested, and strong as a bull, his dark eyes and dark skin flashing, Tuck was tall, muscular but lithe, aggressive and predatory like some kind of agile big cat, his tawny skin and green eyes alive with an intelligence that refused to submit.

Tuck spoke first, his face calm and unblinking, "What are you doing in Hattie's apartment?" His voice was reasonable, yet he clearly expected an answer.

Keon smirked, tipping his chin up slightly. "I'm doing whatever I please, Pretty Boy. Been here more times than I can count." He looked meaningfully at Tuck, his voice grating and combative. "More times than *you*; I can guarantee that."

Tuck remained silent, his only movement a tilting of his head, his expression growing quizzical. He glanced at Hattie, seeming to take in her terrified expression, and then appeared to make a snap decision, as if something had clicked into place inside of him. "I asked you a question." His voice was calm, smooth, and honeyed, and in a strange way, it was vastly more terrifying than Keon's blunt, hard-edged temper tantrums; Tuck was a man fully in control of his emotions, and he wielded that bat with a devastating precision. His voice was so soft, Hattie had to almost strain to hear it, but it was charged with an electric intensity. "And you *will* answer me."

Keon's eyes widened. People down in the PBM did not talk to him like this; they hadn't for quite some time.

He stepped over the threshold, coming to a stop mere inches from Tuck, who still held fast to his position, a look of utter blankness on his face. Though Keon was wider and bigger, Tuck stood slightly taller.

Keon's deep voice sounded like crunching gravel. "I would say let's take this outside"—the slow, dangerous smile of a man who was both accustomed to and seemed to enjoy a certain amount of violence split across his features; he looked down at the walkway where they both now stood and looked back up—"but we are outside." He let the unspoken threat dangle, relishing in the confrontation.

Tuck's voice was bland as he deadpanned, "I am waiting for an answer to my question. Why are you in Hattie's apartment? And why does she not look happy about it?"

Steam seemed to billow out of Keon's flaring nostrils; Hattie had only seen him get so worked up that he was rendered speechless one other time. It hadn't ended well. For anyone.

She extended a timid hand. "Keon, please—"

He ignored her.

This was the moment; she knew it with the certainty of the ground she stood on. She had two seconds—maybe three, tops—to intervene, or there would be no going back. She knew Keon, and once he felt disrespected, it was do or die. There was no other course of action available to him. He was constitutionally unable to work through disagreements in a measured and mature way.

And Tuck—though radiant intelligence gleamed brightly in his eyes, and he was more self-possessed than Keon and his stunted emotional development—she was under no illusions about his upbringing. He was a red-blooded, testosterone-fueled, physical, young, alpha male from South Philly; he might not freak out and lose control like Keon, but to just turn around and walk meekly back down the drive didn't seem like something in his emotional repertoire either.

Dashing forward, she flung herself between the two clashing bucks, giving her body as a sacrifice to slake the passions of men—once again. Why did it always fall to her, to women?

"No, don't! Please, stop!" She threw herself upon Keon's wide chest, tangling herself in tightly against his arms and constricting his efforts to rush forward. "Just stop! Please!"

Twisting her head over her shoulder, her eyes met Tuck's. He stood, his body tensed, but his arms dropping to his sides. His unblinking eyes met hers with a sudden depth of sadness that made her want to scream out.

Keon flailed his arms. "Get off me!" He shoved her rudely to one side, pressing her back against the doorframe. "I said, back off, you slippery ho."

And there it was. This was the Keon she knew. Part of keeping up his image down in the PBM was to treat her like an extra in a rap video—whether that described her character or not. She turned to face Tuck, her face burning, mortified that he was witnessing her being subjected to this. He was hearing her dirty secret: she had been willing to sacrifice her identify, her self-esteem, her autonomy, all for a love that, in the end, wasn't even reciprocated. She was a fraud. She lowered her head.

The coldness returned to Tuck's voice, and his hands edged back up. "Don't talk to her like that."

Keon paused, seeming strangely happy that Tuck appeared to finally be getting riled up. He grabbed Hattie's shoulder roughly, surprising her so that she looked up with a startled cry. "This my baby mama. I'll talk to her however I please, Pretty Boy."

Hattie almost couldn't bear the look that flitted across Tuck's usually composed face. There for just a moment and then gone, it spoke an ocean of emotion: denial, heartbreak, and then the worst part—resignation.

He spoke softly, "I see."

Keon grinned. "That's right, you sorry piece of—"

Tuck stepped forward, his voice sparking and popping as if layered on top of a snare drumbeat. "But that doesn't give you the right to talk to her that way. And it certainly doesn't—" Mid-sentence, he sliced forward like a rattlesnake, scissoring between Hattie and Keon, and he punched Keon's chin so quickly that Hattie could hardly process what was happening.

It was a jab, the precise, whip-like lash of a trained fighter.

Keon's head whipsawed back, causing him to release his grip on Hattie's shoulder and seek stability against the doorframe, his big, beefy body sprawling half-in and half-out of Hattie's apartment, like a boxer leaning on the ropes.

Tuck lowered his fists. "And it certainly doesn't give you the right to push her around either," he finished quietly. He looked Hattie in the eyes, holding her wide-eyed stare with unblinking calm.

"She doesn't deserve that at all—she never did—and she just needs to remember that."

Hattie licked her lips, eyes fluttering and pulse racing, feeling as if she were the one on the receiving end of the punch. He had seen her dirty secret, taken it out, looked at its ugliness, inspected it, and then cast it aside, refusing to accept its existence. She swallowed, straining at the dry lump catching in her throat and forgetting for a moment that Keon sagged backward, moaning beside her.

"What the—" Keon stammered, his eyes glazing over as his hands scrabbled for purchase against the small doorframe. "You, you—" He cocked his head, his eyes slowly focusing in on Tuck as if he were an alien or some mythical creature. "You-you hit me?" His voice was filled with wonder and disbelief.

It struck Hattie that Keon must have advanced further up the PBM hierarchy than she had imagined; he was becoming used to his street reputation doing most of the work for him.

"Now, I will ask you to kindly leave," Tuck said, his usual self-possession back and demonstrated by the iron in his voice.

Keon stood up in some semblance of half-slouched straightness, exaggerating his posture like a drunk attempting to prove he wasn't plastered. "I'm just about to leave anyway; don't you worry about that, Pretty Boy." He paused, frowning. Hattie could almost hear the gears grinding in his head. He tilted his head, looking intently at Tuck as if trying to remember something, and then spoke slowly, the words coming out in a thick-tongued sneer, "But I just got one question for you first." He jabbed a blunt finger toward Tuck, who eyed him with a measure of wariness and curiosity. Keon lifted his chin. "Why are *you* here?"

Reflexively, Hattie latched on to Keon's forearm, shocked that—for maybe the first time ever—Keon seemed like he wasn't going to retaliate. *Maybe he really has changed?* She stood there, slender fingers nestled in the crook of his muscular forearm almost appreciatively, her eyes riveted on Tuck's still form.

Tuck didn't speak, but his eyes drifted to Hattie. She shrugged slowly, curious herself as to why he was here. This seemed to be the wrong thing to do, and a brief shadow passed across his otherwise placid features. His voice was quiet. "Your baby's still, um, okay. And scheduled for transport tonight." His eyes bounced along Hattie's hand, still nestled against Keon's forearm, before she quickly withdrew her hand. Tuck started to turn away, his face pained. "I just thought you should know. And I guess I came at the right time. *Both of you* should know."

Hattie felt a tiny stab in her heart. "Wait, Tuck—"

"No, it's okay. I'm going to go." His eyes, no longer sparkling but bright and shiny pools, like a wounded animal, locked on to hers for a moment of infinities, and then he looked away. "I have to go."

Hattie suddenly noticed that Keon had gone rigid, his large body still.

He turned to look at her, something strange in his eyes. "Hattie? What is he saying? Our baby's still *okay?*"

Hattie swallowed, uncertain of what to say. She felt a slow, squeezing feeling, as if the world were compressing in on her, crushing her one millimeter at a time. Somehow, she was going to make both of them mad at her; she just knew it. "Well," she said, trying to buy some time, "what do you mean—"

"I mean," he interrupted, raising his voice, "I thought you said you had an abortion already!" His voice became frantic, the emotion so strange across his wide, blunt features that Hattie had to hold back a gasp of fear. He stared intently at her stomach, as if he could somehow see inside her. "What do you mean, the baby's *okay?* The baby's not gone?"

Her hand fluttered to her throat as he took a halting step toward her. How could she possibly explain this to him? Her eyes darted to Tuck, now standing frozen on the walkway, half-turned to leave and seeming to loathe placing himself in the middle of a parental spat.

"I did!" she shouted. "I did have an abortion!" The squeezing feeling intensified. "And they took the baby out of me, but it's still, somehow, alive in the womb, just sitting there at MM, all alone." The vise grip seemed to hit a breaking point, and something ruptured inside her, causing her to scream. "And I regret it. Oh, I regret it." Her eyes were wide, panicked and pleading with him to understand. Seeing his mouth gape open at her revelation, she felt equally surprised at what had spilled out of her mouth. But it was true. She had made a mistake, a terrible mistake. "Please, you have to believe me." She began to sob. "I'm sorry. I'm so sorry. I just want her back."

"Her?" Keon said, a look of wonder on his face. "It's a … a …" He swallowed, as if to say it out loud would make it cease to be real. He tried again. "I have a daughter?"

Hattie looked up, meeting his eyes, her voice carefully neutral. "Yes. You have a daughter." She pursed her lips and then said softly, "We have a daughter." Her voice took on a note of wonder to match his own, and she spoke through the tears, looking up at him hopefully, hating herself even as the words left her mouth, "We made her together."

"And you gave her up." Keon's voice became hard and brittle, like a bone splintering in her mouth. "Without even telling me." His eyes became dark and hooded, deadly and dangerous, even with the splash of sunlight illuminating his gleaming skin. "You gave up our daughter, *my* daughter, and you didn't even bother to let me know."

"I told you"—Hattie's voice sounded weak, even to her ears—"you left, not me."

"Well, you had your chance." A vicious sneer curled his lip up, revealing large white teeth. "And you gave her up." He extended a thick finger, pointing right at her breastbone and making her feel as if she were somehow marked in a permanent way. "You don't get a second chance. You already chose. And you gave her away."

The ground felt unstable beneath her feet, and she resisted the urge to pass out. She felt herself sinking, tipping backward into oblivion at the realization.

Here was the plunderer of her body, telling her that she had inflicted the same damage on their daughter's innocent body. He had harmed another body. She had harmed another body. How was she any different than he was? To disregard other bodies as less precious than your own, this was his sin, and now, it was hers. But what about Jane? What had she done? The way Hattie had put her own interests, the safety and comfort of her own body, above that of her grandfather's frail, elderly form, and now Jane's tiny little form. How was that any different than Keon's plundering of her own body?

She fought to keep her balance, her words coming out in a whisper. "Keon, I—"

"We're done." He tipped his chin at her. "Now, I'm going to get my daughter."

Hattie's eyes widened. "You, what?" Her mind raced, trying to remember how much information about MM she had shared with Mrs. T and what Keon might actually know. She swallowed. Enough.

"And, if either of you"—he pointed that thick finger at Hattie and then at Tuck—"goes anywhere near my daughter"—that cocky, streetwise PBM sneer returned to his face, and he turned his finger into the barrel of a gun, miming the shooting of each of their chests—"then I'll kill you."

Shocked silent, Hattie stood breathless as Keon swaggered down the walkway and past Tuck, scraping up against his shoulder with an aggressive slouch.

Hattie spoke quickly before he could get too far away, "But, Keon, why?" She cleared her throat. "Why are you doing this? I never thought—" She choked back a sob. "I never thought you'd want her. Don't do this just to get back at me, please."

Keon turned, slowly looking over his shoulder and back at her, even as he continued to walk away. His voice was calmer, more measured. "You take care of your own, Hattie. That's what we do; that's the PBM way. You know that's what I'm about."

Hearing the *PBM way* lingo, Hattie noticed Tuck stiffen almost imperceptibly. He knew. Everyone in Philly knew. You messed with someone who repped PBM, you messed with all of PBM. The squeezing feeling returned; what had she gotten herself—and now Tuck—into?

She knew that, without a doubt, Tuck was the better choice, but since when was love objective? Since when could you just tell yourself who to care for, who to love?

Keon was still walking away, almost too far away to hear, and she hated herself for even opening her mouth, especially with Tuck so close, standing rigid on the walkway, his features as still and placid as an ice-cold lake, but it just came out.

Her eyes landed on Keon's wide, muscular back, and she called out plaintively, "But what about me?"

For a moment, her heart fluttering like a bird nudging the bars of the cage and finding it had swung open, she thought Keon might stop and walk back to her, but he just glanced at her over one shoulder, a sneer curling his lip, and lifted his eyebrow.

Before turning away, he lifted his finger again and made a shooting motion.

Right into her heart.

Chapter Twenty-One

Just a Simple Procedure

"Do you smell something?"

The voice, so close and yet surprisingly muffled, speaks again, "I could swear, I smelled something. Something like..." A pause. "Like smoke."

Another voice, now heaped with scorn. "Don't be ridiculous; this room is sterilized and completely airtight. If you're smelling anything, it's because you brought it in with you. You aren't smoking again, are you, Biff?"

The first voice speaks again, so soft that I have to strain to hear, "I don't smoke, never have. Not that you would know." A little louder. "And my name's Cliff. I already mentioned that."

"Whatever, Jiff. Let's just hurry up with this, so we can get out of here." The sound of gloves snapping. "This one needs to be prepared for transport tonight. I know this is just a simple procedure, at least for me, and that's why I'm the doctor, and you're not, huh, Griff? So, stop your glowering, and let's get this over with."

The first voice, now suddenly sounding much closer, speaks slowly, "Yes, Doctor. Site is prepped."

"All right then, here we go."

I feel a rumbling pat that seems to shake me all over, making me feel seasick with all the sloshing. I struggle to re-orient myself, and find, to my surprise, everything around me is smooth and slippery and without a foothold or handhold to be found, no matter what direction I turn. Panic slivers through my extremities, causing my heart to beat even faster.

"Not like the old days, huh, Biff? Getting rid of the mother to give us a three-sixty-degree view of what we're doing was the work of genius—*my genius*, of course. Now, it's just a simple procedure."

"Yes, Doctor."

By the tone of his voice, I guess that this isn't the first time he's heard this piece of information. My confusion grows with each moment. I hear an insistent beeping.

"Heartbeat's spiking, Doctor."

Another slight pause, and then the voice speaks again, "That happens when the womb is roughly handled sometimes."

A loud guffaw at the mild rebuke, and I suddenly find myself twisting, swirling, and sloshing around once again.

"Listen here, *Biff*, there's only one doctor here for this procedure, understand?" Another slapping sound, and I'm sent to whirling around and around, growing dizzier and more disoriented by the moment. "If you've got a problem, you can leave. Got it?"

A tiny pause before the voice replies, "Yes, Doctor. Understood."

"Good. Let's proceed. Confirm code."

"Code 468."

"Code 468 confirmed. Syringe with spinal needle."

A pinprick of light is followed by a sharp snap on the base of my neck that I struggle against, but it's too late.

My heartbeat spikes to unimaginably high levels.

All around me, liquid swirls. I taste saline and fight back a retching scream. The sensation of choking threatens to overwhelm me, and I kick out, making contact with that slippery surface again.

The quiet voice again. "I hate this part."

"If I want your commentary, I'll ask for it. Maybe if you weren't a medical school reject, then you could work at a real hospital. Now, shut your trap and give me the speculum. Quickly now, along with the cannula, and set the aspirator to two hundred."

The intrusion of light widens, along with a low-level humming sound. Inexplicably, I feel myself being pulled toward the brightness, and I struggle with all my effort to resist.

"Increase to four hundred."

"Um, Doctor?"

"*What is it?*"

"I think I hear something outside the door. And I still smell smoke."

"Enough about that! *Just do it!*"

My equilibrium shifts, and I ricochet around the wet, slippery surface like a rag doll thrown to the elements. I sputter and choke, willing myself to scurry backward, yet my legs feel weak, and I slip and slide, drawn incrementally toward the insistent tugging. My heartbeat is wild, unrestrained, and I feel as if it might pound out of my chest and cause me to keel over with a heart attack at any moment. And, if that doesn't kill me, lightning shocks of adrenaline course through my veins, borne along by a terrifyingly nameless fear, sending me spinning noiselessly into my own private nightmare.

"Cease aspiration. Size four curette."

Gleaming metal invades, and the pain is so immense, my body convulses. Harsh ridges rake against my skin, instantly debriding it before the pressure subsides.

"Take this. Give me the five instead."

The blinding pain returns, probing and impatient, and then it retreats, accompanied by an agitated sigh.

"Forget it. Give me the forceps and the embryotomy scissors, and be quick about it. We've only got two minutes left for this one if we want to be on schedule. Can't let those blasted TEDs take over every job, eh, Biff? But that's where it's headed if we don't get a move on."

Two sharp tugs, a loud snipping sound, and I feel my world disintegrate.

The last words I hear, "Well, I'll be a drunk monkey's uncle. I think I smell smoke. Biff, why didn't you say something earlier, you dolt? Holy— Biff, this doorknob is hotter than the flames of hell!" A scream pierces the air. "I just burned my scalpel hand!"

I am helpless, adrift at sea.

The pain is gone.

All is blissful, serene. I recognize this sense of betweenness, and it brings me both strange comfort and overwhelming sadness.

I don't know how I know, but *I know.*

I can feel it.

It's come to an end, my time over *there.*

Chapter Twenty-Two

Silent Scream

Hattie stumbled forward, dodging canyons and cracks in the ruptured sidewalk. She felt an overwhelming sense of coming full circle, of returning back to where this had all started, and yet what had she learned?

Step forward, one foot at a time. Right and then left. Repeat.

Her heart still broken, she had discovered that putting all the pieces back together again required an operation far more complex than avoiding the potentially maternal-back-breaking cracks on the path before her.

And yet, still, she pressed on, moving forward with the strength for just one more step, continually replenishing with each stride. And maybe that was the lesson, if even there was one—you just kept going, no matter what. You didn't know how you could possibly continue, but you just took one more step, and the power to take the next one would appear in response.

A flock of midnight-black ravens raced across the gray skies overhead, casting off shadows that flittered across her path with a looming menace as they darted in formation among abandoned telephone wires. A solitary caw was echoed back by a chorus of screams that made Hattie duck, cringing even as she moved faster toward MM. It was a bad omen, and blinding fear raced up her spine. What if she was too late?

As Keon had raced down her front porch and down the street to MM, Tuck had turned to her, his face impassive and his voice cold, and said that it was not uncommon for the baby to be "prepped" pre-transport.

"Meaning?" she had asked, her heart racing.

His voice had been soft and not unkind but final. "That it might already be too late."

And so, she had pushed by him, hurrying down the sidewalk, in a race against the father of her child and her own selfish decisions. She doubted Keon could get in the womb room, but she wouldn't put anything past him. He could be stubbornly creative in that frustrating way that people used to getting their way seemed to have. And, even if he couldn't get into the womb room, she didn't doubt he could cause some serious damage.

Maybe Keon was right though. Maybe she didn't deserve Jane. So what if she had regrets now? Matilda had said it was only natural, and Sally-Anne had echoed the same from personal experience. But so what? Regrets were just feelings, and as she had come to realize with Keon, feelings didn't mean jack; actions were all that mattered.

What kind of mother then was she? And what kind of person? She wondered, thinking of her grandfather and of Tuck. If actions were all that mattered, then to her great surprise, the green-eyed charmer who had so initially repulsed her was fast showing—not saying, but *showing*—that he cared about her, and what had she done in return but virtually spit in his face with her pathetic appeals to her abusive baby daddy, Keon?

She crossed the street and found herself growing sick, even as she drew closer.

Sniffing, her nose wrinkled up in surprise, and she slowed her pace.

Was that smoke?

Dashing around the corner, she stopped, her fingers drifting upward to cover her widening mouth. Directly above MM, surrounded by dozens of running and screaming people, smoke billowed toward the sky, melding with the black clouds, as if in some kind of wicked partnership. Her mouth made a silent scream, and she ran forward, dodging in and out of people fleeing in the other direction.

This was it; she knew it with a strange, maternal certainty. This was her chance to redeem herself and save her baby girl, to prioritize another's body over her own. She would give herself to be burned; she would do whatever it took.

With a grunt borne of sheer panic, she flung the door to the waiting room open with the strength of a mother lifting a car off her child. Sheets of blinding smoke stung her eyes, and she dropped to her knees, instinctively knowing that she would need to crawl the rest of the way. Scrabbling forward, she pushed through the door leading back to the hallway, hastily swiping her card, even as she thought of how foolish this was. And yet, as the door closed behind her, she found that the air in the hallway, surprisingly, was clear of smoke for now and much easier to breathe.

She stood up and, still hunching low, ran toward the womb room.

Just wait, Jane. Your mother's coming.

She ran forward, her mind racing even faster than her feet.

Too late.

Too late.

Her feet slapped sharply against the linoleum floor.

One, two.

One, two.

Too late.

Too late.

Keon's words lanced through her thoughts, cutting her to the quick.

"You gave her up."

"You gave her up."

She bit back a moan, eyes watering from the tendrils of smoke wafting overhead, beginning to grow thicker with each passing step.

"You don't get a second chance."

Maybe he was right. She didn't deserve a second chance—she knew that—and yet here she was. Stumbling forward, she choked on a sudden gust of acrid, pungent smoke that assaulted her wheezing lungs, and she fell to her knees. Still, she crawled forward, finding that, if she kept her chin almost scraping the ground, she could breathe though in ragged half-gasps.

Rounding the corner, she drew up short, feeling overwhelmed by the sudden stab of helplessness. Hot, angry flames danced across the door to the womb room, barring any hope of entering the only entrance. Heat radiated outward, threatening to scorch her eyebrows and hair, even from this distance. Crouching low, she blinked her eyes rapidly against the plumes of swirling smoke that encircled her in its slowly suffocating embrace. Coughing, she pitched forward, fighting the insistent creeping demands of the smoke to enter her and then surround her in a ruthlessly amoral game of divide and conquer.

Her eyes darted back and forth, looking for an opening. But it was too hot. There was no possible way that she would be able to brave the roaring flames guarding the womb room without being burned tremendously, perhaps fatally.

Panic rose within her, threatening to suffocate her even more than the acrid smoke seeping into her gasping lungs. Had she come this far, only to lie helplessly on the floor right outside of where Jane was? Her shoulders slumped; part of her wanted to just remain motionless on the floor and let the flames consume her. What kind of mother was she? A quitter—that was what. Keon's words pierced her heart: *You take care of your own*. If she was being lectured on maternal attachment by Keon, of all people—a self-absorbed and callous taker, who would rather run a hustle on the streets than nurture a baby—then what did that make her? But she was just a lowly lab tech, just starting out. It wasn't that she didn't want to ever be a mother. She just wasn't ready—why, she had just started learning all the equipment when she discovered she was pregnant. If that TED hadn't—

Eyes widening, she crouched motionless before scrabbling backward, as if jolted with a cattle prod. With a manic intensity, she flung herself back down the hallway, crawling as fast as she could toward the inner Medical Ring where all the TED units were housed.

If she could get into a TED unit and whiz back to the womb room in time, she likely wouldn't feel a thing while going through the flames. In fact, even the Philadelphia Fire Department used something similar for search-and-rescue operations, finding it far safer to send a robot into the worst of the flames than a human being. Now, would the medical-grade TED unit retard fire and filter the air and do any other number of things that she was likely forgetting? She had no idea, but she had to try.

With a gasp, she flung herself up from a crouching run and slammed her badge against the reader outside of the cavernous room where she had first received the news from Matilda that she was pregnant. Frantically, she raced toward the nearest

TED station, grateful that the smoke wasn't as bad in this area and that what smoke was there clung like gray rain clouds up near the high ceiling and away from her panting mouth.

Over and over, she slapped her badge against the external reader on the station—it was maddening how slow even this advanced technology seemed to operate whenever you needed it most—and finally, with a tiny chirp, followed by a glowing green indicator light flicking to life, she had access. Tapping furiously, she enabled manual joystick mode. This was one of the first things she had learned from Sally-Anne and some of the other, younger techs; she had known how to race across the enormous room in their weekly TED derby before she even understood all the procedures for checking a patient in and out, and finally—gratefully—it was coming in handy.

As the exterior shell whooshed shut with an airtight click, Hattie put all thoughts of what Matilda would say if she could see her out of her mind. She would worry about that later; now, the only thing that mattered was finding Jane.

Piloting the TED was extraordinarily easy despite any lack of hand-to-eye coordination because the bevy of sophisticated sensors and safeguards practically steered the unit autonomously. As Hattie raced back down the hallway, she realized it practically was fully autonomous. It was a lot like bowling with the bumper pads up; you just aimed in the general direction of where you wanted to go, went as fast as you possibly could, and then relied on all the little automatic course corrections that the on-board microprocessor whirred through in a dizzying number of calculations per second to ensure you ended up where you wanted to be.

As she jerked back on the joystick with a desperate two-handed yank, her face fell as she stared through the visor to see a wall of solid, angry flame sheeting up ahead and blocking the entrance to the womb room. Sharp pings began to alert inside the unit; auditory warnings scrambled insistent commands to retreat.

"Warning! Extreme temperatures detected ahead. Do not proceed."

"Warning! Loss of air quality detected. Do not proceed."

Hattie gritted her teeth, taking a deep breath to calm her jangling nerves. She could breathe just fine now, but she was under no illusions about how long that would remain the case. Her fingertips, slick with panicked sweat, grasped the knob of the joystick, and she said a silent prayer.

This was it.

The moment was here; it was now or never.

She had chosen herself over her grandfather, no matter how she liked to idealize the heroism in his final request, and God help her, she had even idealized her own role in that final act. In the end, it was a cowardly thing she had done—to go along with his selfless plea. He had been thinking about her; she hadn't been thinking about him, only about herself. Wild, clawing regret spiked up her throat, the physicality of it almost causing her to choke and wretch more than any smoke in the air.

And then there was Jane. Try as she might to spin it in a way that absolved her of the tortuous guilt that swirled like black plumes of smoke inside her, she just couldn't. The pregnancy hadn't caused her to sprout an extra pair of arms and legs, something she could choose to get rid of, as if a mere amputation; those crazed Four-Leggers were right about that. There had been another body living inside her. So close and so dependent upon her but entirely distinct. And that other body had needed her. And she had let her down. A sob racked Hattie's body, causing her to clench the joystick even tighter.

She had chosen herself over her grandfather, and then she had done the same with Jane, but now was her chance for redemption. Into the flames and through the fire, she would give herself for her daughter. Maybe Keon was right; maybe it was too little and too late, but it was all she had.

With a sharp intake of breath, she jammed the joystick forward with all her might.

The harsh sound of breaking, scraping, and melting steel exploded as she made contact, whipsawing her back and forth against the TED's internal cushions, giving her an instant, dizzying headache. Bright flashes of light spangled across her vision, her eyes blearily focusing in and out, before she shook her head slowly. She breathed a slow, halting sigh of relief. Nothing felt broken, though she had been rattled around pretty good inside the TED unit despite the array of inflated cushion-like supports all around the interior.

Tentatively, she nudged the joystick forward, and after a worrying moment of whirring gears, some internal mechanism caught, and the unit rolled ahead, crunching over the downed and now-crumpled door. Thankfully, the TED units were made of sturdy stuff; she had been assured of their virtual indestructibility many times during their derby races, and Matilda had told her the exterior shell was fabricated from a kind of space-age polymer. But—Hattie realized with a sharp intake of smoky fumes—being capable of ramming down a door and being able to withstand the immense heat of direct flame, all while keeping an inhabitant breathing clean air, seemed to be far beyond this unit's specs.

She needed to hurry.

Frantically, her shaking fingertips directed the joystick across the room and down the row where she had first seen Jane's womb. Rolling up to an abrupt stop, the unit rocking back and forth, Hattie's heart sank. Her patient number was still brightly lit above the storage rack, but that was it.

Jane was gone.

It was over; they had taken her.

She was too late.

Great, heaving sobs overtook her, and she fought back the urge to wrench the joystick sideways and ram the unit directly into the offending storage rack.

Think, think. What could she do?

Maybe it was time to finally admit the finality of her choice and to live with its consequences. Regret, her silent companion, was now destined to be her mate for life. It was over—

And then, above her sobs, she heard a sound.

It was coming from the back corner of the cavernous room, back where the flames appeared to be the strongest. Slowly, as if in a trance, she pushed the joystick forward. Whether out of desperation, self-immolation, or something else entirely, she didn't know, and yet she continued forward, the gray fumes transmogrifying to thick black swirls that decreased visibility outside the visor to nearly nothing. Still, she pushed forward, the deadness inside urging her onward.

The sounds grew louder. Voices. Shouting—no, screaming. Shrieks that she couldn't unhear. And then she bumped up against something, her head whiplashing forward and then back against the pillowy little cushions behind her neck.

A door.

Jerking the joystick back, she waited for its retreat of a few paces, and then suddenly, she slammed the joystick forward with both hands, a scream escaping her lips that startled her so much, her hands slipped off the controls.

When Hattie awoke—seconds later? minutes later?—she felt a desperate, savage panic that froze her mouth into a silent scream. The TED unit lay upended on the ground with her still inside and the motor still whirring, though it remained as motionless as a coffin, nestled on the remnants of what was once the door and a charred industrial-sized table. The unit was cracked, allowing smoke to seep in and slowly suffocate her. Flames danced just outside the visor, and for a horrifying moment, her mind still trying to process what was happening around her, she imagined she had awakened in hell, the flames ever-consuming inward on her as payment for her sins.

And that wasn't even the worst part; the smell, it invaded her senses, somehow seeming to be more than just a smell, so intense that it was as if she could taste it, see it, hear it, touch it. She fought back a reflexive wretch. It was the smell of something recognizable but twisted in an overpowering and nauseating way. Horror flooded her mind as she slowly looked down to see a blackened lab coat, virtually disintegrated, some sharp-looking metal instruments, and a gleaming gold wedding band. The ring hung loosely on what looked to be a blackened hand—

She bit back a scream, the realization threatening to overwhelm her, for the smell assaulting her nostrils was that of burning flesh. And the worst part—a little once-sealed medical bag, now blackened and melted plastic, looked to contain something like tiny bones. Barely visible through the smoke, she could make out a label on the bag, and squinting through the tears in her eyes, she read something that made her dizzy with heartbreak.

Her patient number.

Once lost, now found, but too late. In stunned silence, she looked at bone of her bone and flesh of her flesh. She had failed her, forsaken her, and now failed her once again. She had been a part of her, sure, but now, looking at the tiny remains, she realized just how much this was a distinct and separate body.

Not her own body, but one of the other bodies, tiny and neglected by those with the power to avert their eyes while conveniently plundering those other bodies for their own gain. Be it convenience or profit, it was all the same. What did motive matter to the body being plundered? Was not the harm to the body just as damaging, just as final?

So what if the tiny body was inside her or not? It was still a separate, distinct body, was it not? She was not that body, and that body was not her. What right did she have to do damage to another body? Even as her mother—no, *especially* as her mother—didn't she have a duty not to harm another body?

Hattie wept.

It was not just any other body; it was Jane's body.

Panic sent her heart rate soaring, and she began to feel light-headed, the combination of the stress and the smoke beginning to take its inevitable toll.

Her eyelids grew heavy.

Blurry at first but then rapidly coming into focus, as if twisting the lens of a camera, her grandfather's tired, deeply-lined face, grizzled with coarse stubble, came into view. His eyes, always so full of light and humor, now drooped with sadness.

The contrast had been so great that day that Hattie bit back a scream of panic upon walking into the living room where he made his bed on the couch, wrapped in quilts and wearing his favorite beige cardigan, always fully buttoned up. His skin had been flat and waxy-looking, dull and lifeless, his normally bright skin now an admixture of beanstalk yellow and dishwater gray.

He had just lifted a tired, shaky hand, clutching her wrist with his long-nailed, bone-thin hand and motioned for her to sit beside him on the couch.

"*This is for the best*," he had said. "*Now's the time*," his weak, whisper-quiet voice had said.

And the worst part: "*I want you to do it. Please, Hattie, it's the best thing for you, isn't it?*"

Even then, in the grip of great pain, he had been thinking only of her. And, curse her, she had hesitated in answering, only offering feeble resistance. She had allowed him to lead her to take the easy way out.

And so, that day, she had done it.

Given him the full bottle of pills, stopped hiding them from him.

He had gone softly, quietly, holding her hand. But the dying look in his eyes had never left her memory, for it was not sadness, nor pain. It was understanding.

In some way unique to the older with the younger, he had known her. Known how a small part of her was relieved he was gone. Relieved that she could have her house back, her time back, her life back. He had taken a toll on her all these years, and the last look had said that he knew it, so it was not without its gratitude, too, but it was an understanding look, a knowing look. It was a look that had said she had a right to finally choose herself over him, but it had broken her heart. She had chosen the temporary comfort of her own body over the safety of these other bodies—first, her grandfather, and now Jane.

Hattie blinked her eyes rapidly, wishing she could just grab her own head and shake loose the unwelcome thoughts that kept intruding. Why now? Why couldn't she, for once, stop thinking about her grandfather? She had managed to keep her secret for two years, but now, the end was here, and it was time to stop lying.

Say it, she said to herself. *Say what you've done.* If she couldn't tell anyone else, at least she would be honest with herself.

She fought back that familiar hot rush of shame.

She swallowed, her throat dry as tendrils of smoke enclosed her trembling body.

Just say it.

Admit it.

She forced herself to mouth the words, even as the smoke swirled closer, *I killed him. I killed my grandfather.*

She had turned her back on him when he needed her most.

Just like Jane.

I'm sorry.

Flames licked around her, hungrily moving inward. Smoke enveloped her, whispering its seductions of sweet relief, and she allowed herself to succumb to its insistent tugging. Her eyes fluttered open once, twice, and then slowly shut. This was what she deserved; why fight it?

Chapter Twenty-Three

Here

My heart's not racing any longer, though the memory of it is so strong that I begin to breathe and pant furiously, my mouth moving in the open-and-close, open-and-close rhythm of a gasping fish. A large hand descends on my shoulder, the touch strong and reassuring but so gentle. And then, as quickly as the feeling arrived, it vanishes.

My eyes flip open, and the golden brightness overwhelms my senses. I blink rapidly, adjusting. I'm still sitting in the chair, the one next to the red button, though for some reason, the button is gone.

"You're back," he says simply.

"Yes," I say, though all I want is to keep looking straight ahead at the rolling hills and plains before me and not incline my head to look him in the eye just yet. "I'm back." *Back here*, I think in my head but don't speak aloud.

He seems to realize I need a moment to gather myself, and the touch of his hand lifts.

After my breathing slows, his voice speaks softly, just over my shoulder, "You're back for good now. Your time over *there* is over."

At last, I turn my head slowly up to look at him, and what I see shocks me.

He's crying.

His great golden eyes, so full of strength and power and now most definitely love, are swimming with tears. A droplet slowly bubbles along an eyelash before it races down his cheek in a long, streaking rivulet, and he doesn't even bother to wipe it away. He just keeps looking at me with that tender gaze.

"I'm sorry you had to experience that all over again, but that's how the red button works." His voice is a deep rumble but still soft. "And it does help with the healing process." His voice grows reverent, quieter. "That's why he has allowed it because his forgiveness is so immense, but we must use his forgiveness to forgive others, and so this knowledge of all that has transpired over *there* is necessary though painful."

A rush of memories, all that I experienced after pushing the red button seemingly so long ago, floods over me, and I feel that heart-pounding sensation of a lack of oxygen once again. I begin to rock back and forth, taking in air. The hand rests gently on my shoulder once again, and I feel myself calming.

"Take your time," he says patiently. "You can do this."

It's coming back to me.

The pregnancy.

The fire.

"I-I'm so sorry." My chest heaves. "I never meant to hurt anyone. I just—oh, I'm so sorry. I never should have had the abortion. And, with my grandfather, I so regret—"

He stops me, his hand still on my shoulder while he crouches down to look me directly in the eye. He speaks very precisely, his eyebrows knitting together in concern, "What did you say?"

"The abortion," I moan, regret washing over me. "I never should have gone through with—"

"Stop," he says firmly but gently. "I've been told this happens sometimes." He takes a deep breath, and the shadows in his eyes give me a fluttery sense of panic. "I need you to listen closely, okay?"

I nod, my mouth feeling so dry that I don't speak.

He locks eyes with me. "Who are you?"

The memories from over *there* swirl around, disorienting me, and I wonder what kind of question he thinks he's asking me.

Frowning, I answer slowly, "Hattie."

He bites back a sharp intake of breath just before I see the hint of distress skim across his eyes. "No," he says slowly, sucking air in through his teeth. "No, you're not."

"But—"

"You are Jane. Your name is Jane." His eyes turn shiny once again. "Hattie is your mother."

My world shifts.

The choking sensation rises again. "I was—"

"Yes," he says.

I continue because I need to say it, "I was aborted."

His eyes are glassy, pooling with more tears. "Yes."

"Hattie aborted me." I pause, trying the term on with a lilt of wonder in my small voice. "*My mother* aborted me. And my name is Jane."

He nods, not saying a word. Maybe it's hard for him to speak, too.

I fight back a panicked shriek, feeling as if my world were disintegrating like ash flung to the wind. *I was aborted.* And even worse: *my own mother* aborted me. I might never forgive my mother for what she did, for what she took from me. I struggle not to hate her. The loss of my future is so immense, I don't know if I can even speak about it yet. I want to scream out in rage at all that my mother stole away from me.

My own mother did this to me; that's what hurts the most. I trusted her. I needed her. And she betrayed me in the deepest, most personal way possible. I depended on her for my very life; *she was my life.* And then she maliciously and intentionally severed that tie. And it's permanent. There's no going back. I stand, speechless and unmoving, at the realization.

On some level, I know I must be in shock, still processing this monumental revelation. As Hattie, there was pain, loads of it, and regret, an insurmountable mountain. But, as Jane, this is a whole new territory. All of my dreams, my memories—Tuck, Keon, even Matilda, Sally-Anne, and, of course, my grandfather—no, my *great*-grandfather. At this, I choke back a sob. It was all a lie. Those memories belonged to my mother; I was only tasting them, experiencing them ever-so briefly while over *there*.

And that's what hurts the most.

Far better to live a life of pain and regret than never to even have the option, to have it so forcefully stripped from you. The damage to my body, so physical and so permanent. I can remember that bright pinprick of light and all the horrendous pain that followed. I still have that memory as my own; that doesn't even compare to the theft of my future. I will never have a boyfriend to love or even to be frustrated with, a friend to giggle or gossip with, a boss to roll my eyes at. My future, all my potential life experiences and memories, good and bad, they were all stolen from me, too.

My body was plundered, my future was stolen, and my choices, they were taken, too.

It strikes me that pressing that button, that was my first real choice. My only choice. That's what hurts the most. Yes, my life was taken from me, control of my body was taken by force and discarded, but it's more than that; my choices were taken from me, too.

I'm wrapped up in a warm embrace, and he pats my back, whispering soothingly, "There, there, great-granddaughter. It'll be okay. I'm here, and you are loved, so loved."

I freeze, pulling myself back as his hands drop to his sides. "What did you say?" My eyes are wide, my cheeks tearstained. The words catch in my throat as I speak softly, asking him again, "What did you call me?"

Through tears of his own, his eyes sparkle and twinkle, and he draws himself up straight. "I called you what you are, one of the many things you are—my great-granddaughter."

I stand rooted in one spot, unable to form words. Finally, I speak, "You? You are—"

"I'm Hattie's grandfather and, therefore, your great-grandfather," he says this proudly, claiming both of us, my mother and me, with more delight and honor than seems possible, and it gives me a strange, warm, yet unfamiliar sense of kinship. He continues, "And you are both deeply loved."

"You-you're my great-grandfather," I say wonderingly, managing to finally spit it out. "And I'm your great-granddaughter." I'm beginning to babble a little bit, still enamored with the sound of the words on my tongue.

"Yes." He laughs. "I've been dying to tell you."

"But why—"

"It's a timing thing," he interrupts with a smile. "That's his way; it's always about the timing. And his timing is always perfect; you'll see that soon enough."

I launch myself into his arms, enjoying the deep burble of laughter in his chest and the warm golden glow suffusing outward from his skin. Slowly, I pull back, looking him deep in the eyes. "And Hattie—" I pause and give a shy smile. "I mean, my mother—" I pause again, enjoying the sound of the title despite all she took from me. "What about my mother?"

His eyes grow serious. "She has a terrible journey ahead of her and many lessons to learn." He gives a sad smile. "But she'll come around. It's all about the timing. I've got faith in his timing."

I look up at him, feeling the tears in my eyes and on my cheeks, as a matching pair with his own.

"What do I do now?" I ask, tears descending down my cheeks in a flood.

Unbelievably, he beams an enormous, toothy smile, and it's as if sunrays are piercing through cloud cover. He pulls himself upright and takes my hand. "I know exactly what you need. It's time."

"Time?"

"Time you meet him." His voice sounds proud, full of life and so strong that, even against any conscious thought on my end, a tiny little seed of something like hope springs up in my heart.

"Him?" I question, not understanding but suddenly wanting to ever-so badly.

"Oh, yes." His pace is quickening, and I have to half-jog behind him, still latching on to his hand, as he tugs me along in an excited walk-skip. "You'll understand in just a moment, believe me."

My heart is beating wildly, maybe even faster than when I first appeared back over *here*, and yet I don't feel tired or winded. It's only as we suddenly slow, approaching a great golden mountain of glowing that

I realize it's from joy. My tear-filled eyes widen with the realization.

"Here we are," he says quietly. And then, extraordinarily, he bows so deep and so low that I know it's not a mere formality but pure, unadulterated worship, and he backs away slowly.

I turn toward the great golden glow, and a man walks forward.

My breath stops, and I feel as if I might die. It's the scariest moment of my existence, and yet it's as if another dimension has opened up before my very eyes and revealed to me everything I've ever wanted. I moan aloud with terror and longing, all in one. Suddenly, I understand the bow. My body feels as if it might melt away like wax, and I fall prostrate on the ground.

A hand—a human hand, a real hand, and yet something so much more—gently caresses my chin and, with just that touch, lifts me back to my feet.

His eyes are bright, shining like the sun, maybe brighter. Amazingly, he laughs, and it's as if the very marrow in my bones is rejuvenating and strengthening, flooding with peace and warmth like amber sap rushing and coursing through a maple to bubble outward. I realize, in that moment, it's exactly what I need.

And then he embraces me.

The strong arms, his hands encircling me, they feel familiar.

It feels like coming home.

Something inside of me breaks, and all the tears come out in a great, sheeting pour, every tear for everything ever gone wrong, so many that I think I can't possibly have that much liquid in my body, and he takes them all, holding me at arm's length. He tenderly wipes them all away, taking them upon himself in some strange way, for he begins crying, too. I'm shocked, but even through the tears and though he doesn't say a word, I know—somehow, I just know—that he knows my pain, every little bit of it, and he understands. And, slowly, he takes it from me, and all I'm left with is sheer, unfettered joy.

An emotion spikes through me like a jolt of lightning, and I'm so shocked by its intensity that I shake in his arms. It's strange. He seems to know exactly what I'm feeling—the betrayal, abuse, and injustice, the destruction and desecration of the body—but he doesn't hold me at a distance, shame me for the strength of the emotion. Instead, he—I almost can't dare to believe it—hugs me even tighter.

Now, here with him, wrapped in his arms, anything seems possible.

Maybe, with time, he can give me what I need to forgive her. But what do I know? I'm still learning. One thing I do know: with him, even the impossible seems possible.

I allow myself a tiny smile as I look up at him.

I'm home.

Chapter Twenty-Four

Full Circle

The space between waking and sleeping thinned. Hattie struggled upward, as if thrashing from deep underwater and failing to break the surface. She heard muddy-sounding voices. Sally-Anne's insistent squawking interposed with Tuck's calm, deep reassurances made for a polysyllabic chorus that rose and fell directly over her. She kept her eyes closed, still fighting to regain her bearings and dreading what she would see when she awoke. Judging by the location of Tuck's voice and the position of her head, she was lying with her head across his lap and her back rudely reclined against the uneven, abrasive sidewalk.

She could still smell smoke. Coughing once, twice, and again, she clenched forward into a little ball, and yet her eyes remained closed. Physically, she seemed fine, but emotionally, she felt as if she were a tangled-up ball of yarn slowly being unwound from the inside out.

A stage whisper from Sally-Anne, very close to her ear. "I think she's waking up."

"Just give her a minute." A hint of annoyance crept into Tuck's voice. "The medic said to let her come to on her own and that she'll likely be very disoriented." Hattie could feel a shifting beneath her neck. "Just back up, will you? Give her some space."

"Okay, okay. Take it easy. I know I didn't run into a burning building to save her like some superhero, so excuse me, but I'm her friend, too, you know."

Hattie fought back a sharp intake of breath. Tuck had saved her? He had risked his life for her?

The defensive note in Sally-Anne's voice turned malicious. "Where'd her *baby daddy* go off to? Leon or whatever?"

Feeling the banded cords of muscle stiffen like rods in Tuck's forearms, Hattie heard him breathe out slowly and then respond, "Keon. His name's Keon." His voice was low, dark, and quiet. "He left."

"He didn't look happy." A strange note of dismay crept into her voice. "I think he'll be back."

Hattie felt a strange flutter in her chest and hoped that Tuck couldn't detect her pulse quickening.

He spoke slowly, "Not anytime soon."

"But sometime."

Hattie felt him nod. "Yes." His chest rose and fell. "Is it true—what they're saying? That he set the fire?"

The breath caught in Hattie's throat, and she forced herself to continue breathing normally.

Sally-Anne's voice was quiet but sharp as a razor. "I don't know. But he came running into the lobby in a rage, all worked up—he wouldn't stop yelling about Hattie and the baby; that's how I found out who he was—and then the fire alarm went off not long after."

"I see," Tuck said quietly.

"The police are investigating." Sally-Anne's footsteps scuffed the pavement. "If he did it, they'll get him."

"But Keon…" His voice trailed off, and then at last, he spoke softly, "Sure, they'll get him." The lack of confidence was barely disguised.

At the mention of his name, the wild, clawing regret resurfaced, almost doubling Hattie over in pain.

Tuck's hand rubbed her back gently. "There now; it's okay. It's going to be okay."

Squeezing her eyes shut, she fought back the tears that threatened to bubble forth. How did she get here? She had chosen herself over everyone she loved: her grandfather and now even Jane, her only daughter. Here, in Philadelphia, the city that ate its young, she was discovering, we were all Philadelphia. While Keon's streetwise bluster might make him a more visible target, was she not just as much a taker as he was? In sharp contrast to Tuck, Keon always chose himself, and that was what had broken her heart, but how was she any different? When it came right down to it, she had only claimed to love her grandfather, but her actions had proven that she would choose herself first. And Jane—her body slumped with resignation—she had discarded Jane's choice and Jane's life for the idol of mere convenience.

"Take your time, Hattie. Take your time." Tuck's hand was soft along her back yet steady. "I'm right here."

Absurdly, she thought of those info materials in the waiting room lobby. They said it wouldn't hurt, but it did. Not physically—they were right about that, for the most part—but among all the pamphlets and manuals and brochures, those glossy little dispensaries of trite, airbrushed MM propaganda, not a one of them had a single warning about this kind of pain. Heartbreak, loss, regret, depression—it was like losing her grandfather all over again. But, this time, it was worse. Her grandfather had pleaded with her. But her baby, what kind of choice had Hattie given her? None. Hattie had taken that choice from her. She fought back a cry.

Being a feminist and being pro-choice was not without its contradictions. The irony of the *my body, my choice* rhetoric was that it denied a choice to half as many females as it gave. Like her baby, the body inside of her body. And the most ultimate and essential of choices was denied: the choice to live or die.

She had thought that what she wanted most in the world was freedom, flexibility, the right to make her own way in the world; that was the dream of feminism, wasn't it? She'd been just one of many to enjoy the fruits of the fight for that right, and it was a good and well-deserved right; it was worth fighting for—but she had come to realize that what she actually needed most was love, connection, to love someone else above herself.

Feeling the warm, secure embrace of Tuck's strong arms around her, something tiny and hard inside her heart melted just a little bit. Maybe the highest ideal of feminism was not to hold the autonomy and equality of the self above subservience to the other but to celebrate the autonomy and equality of others, too—especially our loved ones. Maybe that was the highest ideal of what it simply meant to be human: to rise above the animalist urge for survival of the fittest and to love and care for others as we did ourselves.

Maybe the highest beauty and strength of the woman was that she instinctively knew to prioritize the care of the body inside her body. She had bastardized the noble ideals of feminism—that all bodies were equal and distinct—to ignore the rights of the tiny body inside of her. If every body mattered, if every woman mattered, then what about the tiny female body that had sheltered inside of her?

And, if being a feminist meant believing that we were all equal—different but no less equal—then *how could one claim to stand for women everywhere while refusing to stand for the little one inside of her?*

For a moment—a daring, hopeful moment—the womb room had allowed her to believe the dream that the past was not actually past. But, now, the cold, hard realization of what she had done was settling in. The past *was* the past, and there was no going back. Jane was gone, and she would have to deal with the consequences. For the first time in as long as she could remember, she saw her grandfather's face and moaned a silent, desperate prayer. And this regret—*oh God, help me*—she deserved it, but maybe it was true what her grandfather had often said: maybe God would never turn her away despite what she'd done.

Because now was a time for moving forward.

She opened her eyes.

Author's Note

I didn't want to write this book. I fought it, but the idea kept growing inside of me, and it wouldn't leave me alone. It was a crazy idea, really. But, when I tried to sleep, it whispered to me. When I tried to write something else, it tugged on the peripheries of my consciousness, daring me to look it in the eye. If I were to do so, I knew what it would mean though. Career suicide, most likely. Too controversial. Too ambitious. Delusional, really.

Let's be honest; I'm a middle-aged white guy writing a book about abortion, set in the inner city, and told from the POV of a young girl, all in a dystopian, futuristic America that's eerily similar in many ways to the world we find ourselves in today. Not to mention, there are complicated issues of reproductive rights, teenage pregnancy, feminism, classism, assisted suicide. One could be forgiven for thinking I'm in way over my head.

And then there's the hate mail. If I can be transparent, I like getting emails from my readers at 3 a.m., telling me they stayed up late, reading my books, and then, in all caps, WHEN IS THE NEXT BOOK COMING OUT? Those emails are nice. The emails (and reviews) that are not so nice are the ones where I'm accused of being a lunatic, fundamentalist, backward, woman-hating, white-privileged, out-of-touch cis-male Christian. And those are just the words that I can print. The other adjectives are ... *even less nice*.

But the idea was still there, tempting me, taunting me to look it square in the eye and just describe it for what it was: a hard truth about a hard, broken world. I don't claim to have all the answers, and what answers I might have are not easy. But I think we can do better; we have to do better. I'm a Christian, so the words in the Bible, the words Jesus says, they mean something to me, of course—because *I know him*. I know what he's done for me, given his very body for me—he has made the ultimate sacrifice for all other bodies—and I have the simple joy just to say *he knows me*. And yet, the truth of this idea, it seemed to be so fundamentally basic that we can all agree on it, whether believer or unbeliever, atheist, agnostic, searcher, dreamer, or skeptic.

The hard truth is this: *the body inside your body is not your body.*

That's it. When coupled with the truth implicit in all civilized society—*we don't harm other bodies*—then even the most atheistic naturalist among us has to admit, when we look at the ultrasound—even a young child knows; we all know—*there's another body in there.* Where there was one, now, there are two. So, to delude ourselves into thinking it's just *my body, my choice* betrays a tragic misunderstanding of reality.

To intentionally harm either of the bodies, mother or child, is wrong. Point blank.

When we harm other bodies because they look differently than us or happen to have a different hue and hair from us, that's wrong. When we harm other bodies because they are smaller than us, unable to speak for themselves, and hidden from our sight and our conscience, that's wrong. Let us never forget that racism and abortion have this in common: though insidious in philosophy, they are not mere disembodied ideas; they are not intellectual musings without real-world, real-life consequences. They are both visceral, embodied practices that *harm other bodies.* Backs are flayed, and limbs are severed; teeth are broken, and skulls are punctured; knees are slammed into pavement, and brain matter is suctioned into a vacuum; hands are bent behind backs to be handcuffed, and tiny little appendages are yanked from their sockets and scraped into the trash. Both practices with the end result a world that can continue oblivious into the sunlight of an American Dream built upon the crushed lives of these other bodies.

But what if the pregnancy might do harm to the mother's body? Of course, when two lives are threatened and only one can be saved, doctors must always save that life. But, if it is merely an inconvenience and not life-threatening, then the right to not be killed supersedes the right to not be pregnant. It is reasonable for society to expect an adult to live temporarily with an inconvenience if the only alternative is doing permanent and fatal harm to another innocent human body.

But what about rape, incest, or disability? Since none of these circumstances are sufficient to justify harming another innocent human body after birth, they're not sufficient to justify harming an innocent human body before birth.

The body inside your body is not your body.
We don't harm other bodies.

And, if being a feminist means believing that we are all equal—different but no less equal—then *how can one claim to stand for women everywhere while refusing to stand for the little one inside of her?*

That's the hard truth. I've done my part. I've told the story. I've told the truth. I can sleep at night now.

Can you?

—Joel Ohman

Author of *Other Bodies*

Executive Director, AbortionFacts.com

About The Author

Joel Ohman is the author of the #1 bestselling *Meritropolis* trilogy and when he's not writing then he's probably reading. He lives in Tampa, FL with his wife Angela and their three kids. His writing companion is Caesar, a slightly overweight Bull Mastiff who loves to eat the tops off of strawberries.

If you want to get an automatic email when Joel's next book is released and join the Reader's Group Newsletter for free books and other giveaways then sign up at JoelOhman.com. Your email address will never be shared and you can unsubscribe at any time.

Word-of-mouth is crucial for any author to succeed. If you enjoyed this book, please consider leaving a review at Amazon, even if it's only a line or two; it would make all the difference and would be very much appreciated.